THE LAST SIN EATER

John Kallergis

ISBN: 0692925929
ISBN 13: 9780692925928
Library of Congress Control Number: 2016917928
Wildgoose Books, LLC, Miami, FL

"Gods and beasts, that is what the world is made of."

Adolph Hitler

For my beloved
Annie
How amazing it is to go through life with you.

PROLOGUE

His majesty George the sixth, by the Grace of God, of Great Britain, Ireland and the British Dominions beyond the seas King, Defender of the faith, Emperor of India, sat directly opposite the American President witnessing the Roosevelt charm unfold before him.

"I warn Your Majesty," President Roosevelt said, smiling at the Queen Consort, Elizabeth. "I have an all-American picnic planned for you tomorrow over at Top Cottage, a small cottage we've got on the other side of the property -- hot dogs, hamburgers, apple pie, all the staples."

"I beg of you sir," replied the Queen, pushing her chair back from the table. "Allow me the evening to recover from this meal; it was splendid." Rising from the table she addressed the King. "I wish to retire for the evening."

George the VI had come to his feet and presented his right hand toward the Queen. She squeezed his fingers and his Majesty knew that she was no longer angry with him. She had thawed, throughout the evening meal, succumbing to the President's charm and wit.

They rarely disagreed, but earlier in the afternoon she had been furious with him when he revealed his plans to her. He had decided to confide in the President of the United States, what was a family problem and she, wasted no words in reminding him that they were no ordinary family.

This dinner, at the President's personal residence was the culmination of their majesties first-ever visit to America. George the VI was the first reining British monarch to visit the United States. The welcome given by the American people was both unexpected and overwhelming, but the greatest surprise was the instant kinship he had developed with Roosevelt. In Roosevelt, he had found a kindred spirit: he was disabled.

The King's speech disorder was his constant battle to fight and in Roosevelt, he had met a man who had to fight to walk. The President had even made a joke about it when he told the King that he could not walk and his Majesty could not talk but together they would have to walk the talk for freedom's sake.

Releasing the Queen's hand, the King turned toward Mrs. Roosevelt. "You are a most gracious host and we thank you for opening your home and your heart to us."

"Thank you, your majesty," Mrs. Roosevelt replied. "It has been our great honor. Goodnight, sir. Come, my dear," she said, taking the Queen's hand.

"Let's leave the boys to their smelly cigars and cognacs. I have a feeling these two will be up all night." Turning to her husband she spoke. "Good night Franklin. Now, don't keep his majesty up to all hours."

As the ladies left the room, the King thought about how much he admired his wife. She was the rock of their family but he often wondered if she would have married him if she had known he would be King. The probability was so remote of his ever-becoming King; the matter had never been brought up for discussion.

Life, along with his wife and two young daughters, Elizabeth and Margaret, had been the happiest days he had known. Until his petulant brother abdicated the throne for love.

It was, after all, unfathomable, to give up rule of a quarter of the world's people, over a woman, but his brother had done just that and he had become King almost overnight.

The President pushed his wheelchair back from the table and started rolling himself to the door.

"Come on James," he said to his valet. "Let's open that bottle of Cognac I have been saving and break out those Cuban cigars. I want his majesty to have a real Cuban cigar …then he'll know why cousin Teddy invaded that damned country in the first place."

The King turned as the President rolled himself by and His Majesty instinctively grabbed the back of the President's chair and guided him down the hall towards the library. This simple act surprised the King himself. He would have never done something like that before today. George VI grew even more confident in his decision to enlist the President's help.

Roosevelt had a wooden ramp built into the house to accommodate his wheelchair. His study was at the other end of the house and down a few steps. The King rolled the President down the ramp and into a large rectangular room painted in a light creamy green and filled with books from wall to wall. There were several overstuffed chairs and two long sofas. Another set of big oversized leather chairs faced a dormant fireplace on the far end of the room.

James had already opened the President's private humidor and was clipping the ends of the Cuban cigars when the President propped his chair up against a small table. James, busy setting up the glasses, placed an ashtray on the table.

The King took a seat in one of the overstuffed armchairs while James served the President and then the King. Both men let their cognac sit as the valet handed them cigars.

Taking the cigar in hand, the King rolled it in his fingers feeling the texture of the fine almost linen like paper that wrapped the tobacco. He put it up to his nose and inhaled. There was something about the smell of leaf tobacco that was intoxicating. James offered a light and the King bent his head down and placed the tip of the cigar into the flame until the tip was lit. He sat back and pulled on the cigar until the burn was even.

Exhaling a blue cloud of smoke, he thought about how much he truly loved smoke. The two men sat back silently smoldering.

After several moments, the King cleared his throat and addressed Roosevelt.

"Mr. President" he said, hesitating. "There is a personal matter, a family matter, which we choose to entrust you with."

Roosevelt shifted in his chair, placing his cognac and cigar down. With a wave of his hand, James quickly disappeared from the room.

The King leaned forward in his chair and spoke in a hushed tone.

"My government knows not of what we are about to ask sir but they are aware of the difficulty and a decision has been made. Our brother has become a problem," The King said, breathing a sigh of relief. He had done it. He had said out loud, that one terrible thing that he had kept bottled up. Feeling a sense of liberation, his words flowed faster and clearer.

"Since his abdication he has not done well. We fear for his personal safety and worry that he is easily influenced by the wrong 'sort'. We have had discussions with the Prime Minister and plans have been made to appoint our brother to a post that will keep him and harm away from each other." Sitting back in his seat, the King continued.

"As our difficulties mount with Herr Hitler -- and mount they will -- our brother will be appointed Governor General of The Bahamas, for the foreseeable future."

The King relaxed in his chair, and took a pull off of his cigar.

The President cleared his throat and spoke.

"How may I help your Majesty?"

Sliding forward in his chair, the King placed his face a little closer to The President's. He opened his mouth but nothing came out. After a moment, he found his voice.

"Our brother does not wish us well. He feels he was railroaded into abdication and we daresay that our father would have been all for it. There are, Mr. President, some, shall we say, sibling rivalries but he is after all our brother and we must protect him at all cost."

The King paused and took a sip of his cognac before continuing, "We need your help in just that Mr. President. We need your help protecting our brother. The threats are many and varied from without and from within. He will be on your side of the world and we are asking you for assistance in keeping him alive."

George VI could sense that Roosevelt appreciated the courage of his words.

"Of course sir, you will have my help," the President said, picking up his cognac. "Governments come and go but a brother, well a brother is forever, and rest assured your Majesty; we understand family

CHAPTER ONE

Tuesday June 4th, 2013
Brentside High School, London, England

Nicholas Ratzenberger stood at the front of his classroom waiting for his students to return their books to the shelves at the back of the room.

"Right, hurry up now, we only have a few minutes until the dismissal bell rings and I need you all back in your seats," he said, raising his voice to be heard above the din.

"What are your plans for the summer, Mr. Ratz?" The question was from Jeremy, one of the smaller boys in the class.

Nicholas smiled before answering. Jeremy was one of the few students he liked. The boy was conscientious and aware, unlike most of his form five class, whom he found to be silly and immature. School would be letting out for the summer in another week and Nicholas dreaded the idea of not having a paycheck for the next three months.

"Well, the life of a teacher is one of wretched poverty Jeremy," he replied, moving to the chair behind his desk. "So I won't be going anywhere on holiday this year."

"That's too bad," Jeremy continued." What about your book? You haven't mentioned it lately... Are you still writing it?"

The great book, he thought. He had started writing a novel over a year and a half ago and had mentioned it to his students in an attempt to teach them something about setting goals and self-determination but it wasn't going very well. "I imagine I will be working on it during our break but, honestly, I haven't touched it in months," he replied.

"Nevertheless sir, you should try to finish it, I would love to read it when you get done," Jeremy said, taking his seat in the front row.

"Thank you, Jeremy. You'll be one of the first to get a signed copy when it's done," Nicholas said, standing and raising his voice to address a group of boys who were taking too long to file their books away. "Gentlemen, I will not ask you again. Take your seats, class has not been dismissed."

His tone had the desired effect of getting all of the students back into their chairs. Nicholas found himself thinking of the small flask he kept hidden in his lower right desk drawer. He couldn't recall if he had taken the last swig at lunchtime, but he was hoping some vodka remained.

Years ago, on his first day, a retiring instructor told him that vodka didn't smell on your breath.

"Drink Vodka," he said. "The little bastards can't smell it, and you will get through the day without killing one of them."

Some days were tougher than others, and Nicholas imagined that it was probably like that in every job. In his case, disillusionment, and disconnect, had settled in.

He was only 29 years old, but it might as well have been 100. His students' constant desire for social interaction and need for instant gratification was such a stark contrast to his existence. He lived well below his means and had practiced the art of delayed gratification for so long; he had begun to believe his day would never come.

The dismissal bell rang promptly at 3:15. As the students shuffled out, Nicholas sat down at his desk to grade papers.

Focused on his work as he was, he hadn't noticed the older woman who had entered his classroom as the students filed out.

She stood directly in front of his desk. "Good afternoon, Mr. Ratzenberger."

Nicholas jerked back, startled by the interruption.

"Oh, you gave me a fright," he said, pushing his chair back and coming to his feet. "I'm sorry I didn't see you standing there; you startled me."

"I apologize. It was not my intent to frighten you. Allow me to introduce myself. My name is Katherine Blackwood. May I sit down?"

"Please of course," said Nicholas, indicating a chair opposite his desk. He immediately realized that Katherine Blackwood was a cut above the regular parent: she was impeccably dressed in a pressed, dark blue dress with a white collar and a simple strand of white pearls around her neck. Her hair and makeup were flawless, and although evidently older, Nicholas could see that she was an attractive woman who still maintained a youthful face and held herself with a certain grace.

Katherine looked around the room for a few moments and then set her attention directly on Nicholas. He immediately felt a little unnerved as her eyes settled on him and he felt an instant almost hypnotic effect.

He could feel her studying his face and he mumbled a little unsure of himself, "How may I help you?"

"It is I who am here to help you, Mr. Ratzenberger."

"Please call me Nicholas, or Ratz, if you'd like. Mr. Ratzenberger is my stepfather and he has grey hair and complains a lot," Nicholas said, hoping some attempt at charm might shake his feelings of intimidation.

A little smile creased her lips, "I'll call you Nicholas. That is what your father named you and that is what I will call you."

Sitting forward in his chair, he locked eyes with Katherine.

"You knew my father?"

"Indeed I did," Katherine replied, in a soft voice.

Nicholas continued to study Katherine's face. This was odd, he thought. This woman was obviously out of place, had gone out of her way to find him and had wasted no time bringing up his father, Andrew Stone, someone he vaguely remembered and never really knew.

"Well, if you knew my father, then you know that I didn't," he said, sitting back in his chair eying this mysterious women, "So, how may I help you?"

"I did know your father and in fact, I loved him very much," She answered. "There is much I can and will tell you about him. I don't know what you remember or what you have been told, but let us start with the fact that your father was a great man who provided a great service to his country and you should be proud to be his son."

Nicholas hesitated before speaking. She had said that she loved his father. His father; the man had become a ghost in his mind. He looked a little deeper at this woman in front of him. He couldn't recall anyone that he knew who had known his father, other than his mother, and she had refused to speak of him for years.

"I appreciate those kind words but the only thing I know is that my father was never around. I remember him vaguely but then he just stopped being and we, well we moved on. I honestly don't think of him much and when I do think about him, I find that I get a little sad. I'm sure that I am curious, but understand, I'm a little cautious."

"I understand," replied Katherine. "I'm planning to tell you everything, but first I must tell you that filling in the blanks about your father is only part of the reason I'm here and I ask for your patience." She opened her purse and continued, "I'm going to give you something and ask that you read it and that you come to my home tomorrow. I have much to tell you and I ask that you respect the process I choose to tell you what it is that I need to tell you."

With those words, Katherine stood up and placed the envelope, she had retrieved from her purse, face down on Nicholas's desk.

Nicholas rose from his seat.

"My address is in the envelope. Please be at my home tomorrow afternoon at 4. I trust that the contents of this envelope will pique your curiosity and you will want to know more.

"Do not be late," she said, turning toward the door. "I do not tolerate tardiness."

As she exited, Nicholas sat back down in his chair dumbfounded. He was experiencing a rush of childhood memories and at the same time, feelings of being scolded by his first primary school teacher.

He hadn't thought about his father in some time. He had wondered about him much more when he was younger but he had stopped asking his mother about him after she married Joseph Ratzenberger. She wanted and deserved a new life, she had told him, and Joseph was willing to adopt him. Joseph Ratzenberger was his new father not Andrew Stone, and that was that she had said.

He turned the envelope over and read the words typed in bold letters, on the other side.

Thomas Nash - 1941

Nicholas opened the envelope, removed the pages inside and began to read.

CHAPTER TWO

Thursday July 17th, 1941
Military Corrective Training Centre
Colchester, England

Thomas Nash stepped out of the Glasshouse, and into a hot rain. He took three deep breaths before turning and looking back at his prison, the irony of the nickname for the place, The Glasshouse, was not lost on him and smiling he started walking into town.

They gave him three months off for good behavior. He had served nine months of a one-year sentence and had been informed that he would be dishonorably discharged from His Majesties Armed Services. Apparently, striking a General was frowned upon.

The rain matted his blond hair to his brow and he discarded his hat, welcoming the downpour as a cleansing from above. He walked out of the complex and down into the town of Colchester dressed in an old pair of black trousers and a grey shirt. An old green military standard issue overcoat was draped over his shoulders. His meager personal possessions were gathered in the bag he carried in his left hand. It was amazing that a lifetime could fit into a single duffle bag.

'The Prince's Head' was located half way down Culver Street, just off the market square. Thomas stood outside for a few moments smoking a cigarette under an overhang from a shop across the street. It was a little past two in the afternoon and few people were out.

He took a last pull on his cigarette, tossed it aside and exhaling, crossed the street and entered The Prince's Head.

It was a relatively large pub and as his eyes adjusted to the light he could not help from thinking back to the last time he was in a pub and General Anderson's chin had struck his fist.

"The Prince's Head" could have been any pub in any town in Britain. Thomas's training and instinct took over as he entered immediately sizing up the room, spotting his sight lines and exit-ways.

A dark wood bar ran the front of the room and then turned and wound off to the back. There were tables and chairs, arranged for seating off to the right and from top to bottom the walls were covered with flags, banners, ribbons and trophies; Many trophies.

There were only a few people in the pub at this hour. A couple of old veterans sat off in a corner nursing drinks and smoking pipes. A young waitress was cleaning up a table close to the front of the bar as Thomas walked in.

"Good God man, ya look like ya drowned," she said, noting Thomas's water logged condition. "Take a seat and I'll get ya a towel."

"That's very kind of you," Thomas said, smiling at the first woman he had seen in a year. "May I ask if Mr. Christie is available?"

"Oh he's in the back," the young girl replied. "I'll fetch him if you want; whom shall I say is asking for him?"

"His nephew Willy told me to look him up," he replied.

"And your name," she asked, eyeing Thomas directly.

"Nash, Thomas Nash."

As the waitress started towards the kitchen, a stocky barrel chested man of about sixty years emerged from the back of the pub. He wore what little hair he had combed back and on top of his white shirt and black pants, he wore a barkeep's green apron.

"Christie," the waitress called out. "This is Mr. Thomas Nash and he's askin for ya."

"How can I be of service to you?" asked Christie, approaching Thomas from behind the bar.

'Well ah, your nephew Willy suggested I call on you once I got out and I thought," Thomas's voice trailed off.

"Nash, you're Nash!" Christie said, extending a meaty arm over the bar grabbing Thomas's hand with his and shaking it. "Let me pour you a drink lad," he said, finally releasing his grip. "Sit down, sit down," motioning Thomas to a seat, "What will you have Lad?

"Just a pint would be fine," said Thomas, sliding onto the barstool.

Christie poured out a pint of dark beer into a mug, topped off the head and placed in in front of Thomas.

"Drink up lad; your first day of freedom!"

Thomas shifted in his seat, a little uncomfortable with the over joyous welcome he was receiving.

"What about you, sir?" He asked, taking his mug in hand. "Won't you join me?"

Christie crossed his arms and laughed, "Never touch the stuff myself, did once, got drunk…woke up married …wretched thing, alcohol."

Thomas laughed and nodding his thanks to the burly 'bar keep', took a long drink from the first beer he had tasted in a long time.

"Willy was very impressed to make your acquaintance, while you were eh…confined," Christie said, wiping down an imaginary spot on the bar top. "He said you might be in some need of work, you know, once you got out."

"Your nephew was the only person I ever came in contact with. That was during my exercise time, three times a week," Thomas replied. "He's a good lad, got me talking and everything."

"Ya mean they had ya in solitary confinement, the whole time?"

"They let me out three times a week for an hour's exercise and your nephew was the only guard posted in the yard to watch me walk about."

Christie looked on.

"Well, Willy kept insisting I talk to him. He told me I would lose my ability to speak if I didn't use my voice and after a couple of months, he wore me down."

Christie broke out laughing, "He's a good egg that Willy, a good egg."

"He was actually right," Thomas replied. "He got me talking and I realize it helped me stay in my skin. I'm grateful to the bugger actually."

"I didn't realize they took it so serious… I mean, solitary confinement. What were they afraid of?" Christie said.

Thomas smiled to himself before answering:

"The army operates on discipline, rules and regulation. They cannot be seen as tolerating any insubordinate action."

"Humph," Christie grunted, folding his arms. "I served in the last one mate. I understand what ya mean;

the buggers are truly committed to their discipline. But it feels good to put it to 'em every once in a while, eh?"

"I suppose it does," Thomas said, enjoying the older man's personality.

"Tell me the true story," Christie said, leaning over the bar and lowering his voice.

"What?" Thomas asked, hesitating. "You mean the General Anderson business?"

"I want to know exactly why ya did it tell me how you popped him one?"

Thomas sat back for a moment gathering his thoughts. Willy had been his only human contact during his incarceration and he had opened up to the boy as to the reason for his confinement. The lad had a deformed right leg and this disability kept him out of active service. Willy still looked at war as gallant, romantic, and irreverent. Thomas's story fit the bill.

He was beginning to see that his tale might have been told once or twice around this pub. Christie was leaning against the back bar, arms folded in definite expectation of the truth.

"It was Dunkirk," Thomas began. "It was because of Dunkirk. The whole damn force had been decimated. The few French troops that were with us were in just as much of a jam as we were and as I waited on that damn French beach for my turn to be evacuated I decided I'd had enough."

Thomas paused and took a sip form his beer.

" For three days the Germans strafed the beaches. We were sitting Ducks burrowing as deep as we could into the sand in a lame effort to protect ourselves. There were injured and dead soldiers scattered all over that beach and the air was a mix of burning rubber and death. In all my days, I can't remember any that dark. "

Christie leaned in to the bar in almost reverent anticipation of some great gift.

"It still mystifies me to this day why Hitler didn't just wipe us out on that beach. We were trapped and all because of the ineptitude of our leaders," Thomas continued. "Me and several of my men had to tread water for almost a half a day waiting for a boat to make its way to us. Finally, on the third day a small harbour vessel came upon us and they hauled us aboard and they got us back to Dover."

Shifting in his seat, he looked the barkeep straight in the eyes: "Imagine what the results would have been if Churchill hadn't roused the British people into saving us. The damned military leadership had stranded us on a beach with absolutely no plan for getting us out. The people, in their small crafts, harbour-boats, fishing vessels -- even small dinghies -- braved the channel crossing to get us out. Not the brass, the people."

Christie was fixated.

Thomas took another long sip before continuing. "I came ashore with a lot of rage. The mistake wasn't made at Dunkirk ... No, it is an institutional mistake," his voice rising. "The damn system of class and privilege had saddled us with inept leaders and I had decided to do something about it."

Christie grunted his disdain at the mention of the ways of the officer corps.

"I came ashore on fire and I found General Anderson, who had been my commander in France, and smacked him right in the mouth."

Thomas sat back in his barstool.

Christie was momentarily dazed. The story had ended too soon.

"That's it…you just found the General and smacked him?"

"Well, it was a little bit more than that," Thomas replied.

Unfolding his arms, Christie held the palms of his hands up as if asking to receive some more.

"Well, I came ashore and found the good General holding court in a local pub, surrounded by his fawning staff. Upon seeing me enter the pub, he called me over and offered me a drink and a seat at his table. As if we had something to celebrate." Thomas shifted in his seat aware that the conversation was stirring some irritation in him. "I openly laughed in his face and told him I would rather drink with the dregs of society before I would ever share a drink with the likes of him." His reaction was disbelief and shock, at first, and he mumbled something about insubordination. I told him to sod off and that he was a disgrace to the uniform and to Britain. He rose from his seat, and at that moment and I offered him the opportunity to step outside. I believe he thought I was joking. Then I asked him if he wanted to remove his glasses so that they would not be broken. He seemed to take this question a little more seriously and then asked me if I had gone mad." Thomas sat back in his chair before continuing, "To be honest, I don't remember any conversation after that, I just remember sinking my fist squarely into his face. I have to say that it felt great."

Christie shook his head up and down having enjoyed those last few details Thomas had thrown in. "Bloody bastards," he said. "A smacking he won't soon forget, eh."

Thomas drained the contents of his glass and placed the empty on the bar.

"Another pint?" asked Christie.

"No, thank you," Thomas said, reaching for his billfold.

"Your money is no good here lad," Christie said, raising his right palm toward him. "Tell me, Thomas. Have ya any plans, places to be?"

"Not really," he replied.

Christie drew another pint of beer and slid it in front of him. "Well, if you don't mind me being a little forward, I could use some help around the pub. I can't pay ya a lot but I do have a room upstairs ya can have and you'll get three meals a day out of the kitchen."

Thomas looked out the window at the falling rain. He really didn't have any other option. He had no family and the military had been his life for the last 18 years. Those days were obviously over.

"I can't guarantee how long I'll stay," he said, turning back to face the barkeep.

"Not to worry lad. Ya stay until ya don't want to stay anymore," replied Christie.

Thomas stood up from his stool and extended his hand.

"I accept your offer sir, and I appreciate your kindness."

"Think nothing of it lad. Any man who smacks a General is welcome here."

Christie let go of Thomas's hand and walked towards the back of the pub, "I'm going to get ya some real food.

"That prison rot will kill ya."

CHAPTER THREE

Thursday June 5th, 2013
Katherine Blackwood's Home
Wycombe, England
30 miles Northwest of London

Walking up the gravel driveway toward the front door of Katherine Blackwood's home, Nicholas admired the stateliness of the Tudor-style. Red and yellow flowers bloomed in boxes that hung below the oversized windows. The English and their gardens, he thought to himself, smiling.

He had not slept well the previous night and had stumbled through his classes earlier in the day. Reading the narrative Katherine had left him was interesting, but he failed to make any connections.

Thomas Nash, who the hell was he? And what did he have to do with his father? Nicholas couldn't recall if his father had even been born by 1941.

Katherine's visit had stirred up long suppressed feelings. Her words had dislodged childhood memories and he spent the night tossing and turning as hazy images of his early childhood filtered in and out of his mind.

He straightened his tie and knocked on the front door. Several minutes passed. As he reached up to knock again, the door opened and an elderly black man stood before him. Amid the well-worn creases on the old man's face were the bluest eyes Nicholas had ever seen.

"Miss Katherine," the man announced over his shoulder. "You have a visitor."

He stepped aside to allow Nicholas to enter and Katherine appeared behind him.

"Good of you to be on time," she said. "I see you got my point."

"You made yourself very clear," Nicholas replied, entering the house and removing his coat. "I felt like a student back in school and you reprimanded me for something I had not yet done."

Nicholas caught the slight smile on Katherine's face, as she turned and walked further into the house.

"Give your coat to Franklyn," she said over her shoulder. "And join me in the sitting room."

Nicholas removed the envelope she had given him from his coat pocket and again was struck by the brightness of Franklyn's blue eyes.

He followed Katherine through the foyer and into a brightly lit hallway. The white walls were lined with paintings of British country hunting scenes. Men in red coats on horseback with their noses held high as if to show their superiority to the mongrel servants and dogs at their feet. Nicholas paused for a moment to look at one of the paintings and admire the quality of the work, even though he had no ideas as to the merits of oil painting.

Katherine stood waiting in front of a set of dark mahogany doors and Nicholas scurried to catch up. "Sorry," he said, with a grin on his face. "Just appreciating the art work."

Katherine opened the doors and led the way into the sitting room, which stood in sharp contrast to the bright and white gallery he had just walked down. The room was wide and lined on three sides with dark oak bookshelves. A large Persian rug of maroon and gold coloring covered most of the polished dark wood floors.

Looking around, Nicholas noticed that every shelf was occupied by a book or newspaper, yet everything was in complete order. Two oversized windows on the far wall had their drapes drawn back. Natural light filtered through.

On the opposite wall to the entrance, there was a break in the bookshelf and a large stone fireplace lay dormant. Two well-worn dark brown leather chairs sat on either side of a rectangular coffee table and a bright yellow leather love seat faced the fireplace. Nicholas could not help but think how out of place the love seat seemed.

Displayed on top of the marble mantel were two silver picture frames. One held a black and white photograph of an older balding gentlemen and the other a color photograph of a 1970 red Triumph Spitfire, with the top down. Nicholas was immediately drawn to the picture of the car.

"I can't believe you have a picture of this car on your mantel," he said, his voice rising. "This is one of my favorite cars of all time."

Katherine had taken a seat in one of the overstuffed leather chairs without responding to Nicholas's enthusiasm over the Spitfire. She indicated to him to take the seat opposite her.

Placing the envelope on the coffee table, Nicholas couldn't shake the feeling of Katherine studying his every motion.

"You have a lovely home. This room seems very warm," he said, as he settled into his chair.

"It was my grandfather's house; that is him on the mantel," she said, indicating the picture of the balding man. "I've lived here since I was ten years old."

"So you have always lived a splendid lifestyle?" Nicholas asked.

"I'm not quite sure what you mean," Katherine answered.

"This house, this neighborhood, it reeks of money. If you spent your whole life here, then you have always had money." Nicholas wasn't quite sure where his line of questioning was coming from, but he felt a bit cocky and he didn't quite understand why.

"Money does not always equate to splendor or comfort for that matter, but if it were any of your business, which it is not," she said, in a stern voice, "the answer is yes. I have always had money." Leaning forward in her chair, she continued: "But I would have given up all of the money to get back some of the things I lost. You will learn as all young people do, that there are some things more important than money."

"I always hear that same line," Nicholas began. "And it's always from people who have money. It's hogwash, if you ask me. People like you always say that money doesn't make you happy, but that's because you have it."

"People like me," she said, lifting her nose up in the air, "Well people like me are correct. Money does not make you happy but it does make you happier."

Nicholas was stunned by the simplicity of her statement. Even the most miserable person would be happier with a million pounds or dollars in their pocket, he thought.

A light knock on the door and Franklyn entered the room carrying a large tray. "Tea, Miss Katherine."

He set the tray on the table between the two sofas and served them both. Franklyn dropped a lump of sugar into each cup, placed them in front of Nicholas and Katherine, shot a glance in Nicholas's direction and then left the room.

Katherine lifted her tea and sat back on the sofa.

Nicholas sipped his tea wondering how long he'd be able to remain patient with the enigmatic Katherine. "Honestly, ma'am, I don't know anybody today who has a black manservant."

Katherine began to laugh, "Franklyn...Franklyn is no servant. Franklyn is family. He came to live in this house in January of 1942 and was here ten years before I arrived. He is 88 years old and except for the first 16 years of his life, Franklyn Gibson has lived in this house."

Katherine began coughing almost the moment those words left her mouth. She got up quickly and moved to the left of the room, disappearing into a small bathroom that Nicholas had not previously noticed.

The break gave him a few moments to gather his thoughts. Getting up from his seat he spent a few moments admiring the photo of the red Spitfire. Katherine walked back into the room.

"My apologies, my throat got a little dry. I needed to get some water.

Nicholas made no mention of the fact that Franklyn had left two full glasses of water on the tray with the tea service.

They returned to their seats and Katherine asked, "How much do you know about the Bahamas?"

What an odd question, Nicholas thought before replying. "I know it was a British Crown Colony off the coast of Florida, independent now, I think. I don't really know that much, in all honesty."

"That's all right," Katherine replied. "It really is the loveliest place on earth, though I've never set foot there. I've seen pictures and had first-hand accounts of her beauty and charm relayed to me," she paused. "And then again, there's Google Maps. I have surfed the world, as they say."

Nicholas's amusement must have shown on his face because she immediately resumed her schoolteacher demeanor. She didn't look the Google type; he decided, best not to judge a book by its cover.

"I do hope you know your British history a bit better."

"I hope so, for my sake," Nicholas replied, grinning at her.

"Very well," she continued, "When you were in school, and certainly as a teacher, I would hope that you studied the abdication crisis that this country endured in 1936 and the subsequent years leading up to World War II. Some say that Edward's abdication was the single greatest act of love ever professed, others, the most ridiculous thing a man has ever done."

She paused for a few moments before continuing. "The truth probably lies somewhere in the middle, but that is up to the writers and the poets to wonder about. Here is what is ultimately true."

Sitting forward in her chair, Katherine's voice grew stronger. "Edward regretted his decision almost from the start and immediately began his slide into treason."

Treason, Nicholas thought to himself. What was this all about? He hoped his confusion didn't show. He thought he had come here to learn about his father and instead he was receiving an abstract lesson back in time, fright with a conspiracy and all. Maybe she's crazy, he thought, and then he remembered.

"I remember it now. I remember it. Edward was appointed Governor General of the Bahamas during the war."

Katherine smiled, "Well done, but the question is, why the Bahamas?"

Nicholas had no answer. He was still trying to tune into what she was talking about.

"Because the Bahamas is on the other side of the world and in 1941, a very isolated spot," she pronounced. "And that is exactly where Mr. Churchill wanted him." Looking directly at Nicholas she said, "1941, that's where it all began."

"Where all what began?" Nicholas asked, bewildered.

"It was where my education into the true ways of the world began," Katherine replied. "Where I learned about honor, and courage, and service."

Nicholas ran his left hand through his hair and slapped tapped his right cheek rapidly with the fingers of his right hand in an effort to wake himself up.

"Are you all right?" she asked, obviously puzzled by his behavior.

"I'm just trying to grasp what it is you are speaking about," Nicholas said. "I mean, Edward VIII, abdication, the Bahamas. What are we talking about? You must have been an infant in 1941. How could your 'education,' as you put it, have begun then and what does any of this have to do with my father?"

Nicholas noticed her reluctant smile as soon as the words tumbled out of his mouth, feeling as if he had pushed too hard. "I'm sorry, I didn't mean to come across so harshly," he mumbled.

"That's quite all right," she replied quietly. "I've seen that 'flash' before," she sat up in her chair and continued. "We are going to spend some time together, you and I, we will probably get on each other's nerves from time to time."

"Thank you for letting me off the hook," Nicholas said.

"What happened in 1941 in the Bahamas has everything to do with your father," Katherine began. "My grandfather documented down to the last detail the events that occurred there in the autumn of 1941 and it was the lessons of those events that shaped the man your father became."

"My father was I think, one year old in 1941," Nicholas said.

"He was two," she replied, relaxing back into her chair. "In 1941, a series of events played out in the Bahamas in which his royal majesty Edward VIII, the former King, and, that woman, were proven to be complicit in a most horrible conspiracy. A reprehensible plan that had it succeeded would have changed the outcome of the war."

"That woman?" Nicholas asked. "You mean Wallis, Wallis Simpson, The Duchess of Windsor?"

"As I said," Katherine replied through clenched teeth, "that woman."

Nicholas could feel the iciness, "can you not say her name?"

"Her name is not worthy of mention."

Nicholas sat up in his chair, "Are you one of those elitists who believe she was a commoner and unfit to marry a King?"

"I will not be trapped by your quick wit Nicholas," Katherine replied. "I am not one to judge anybody when it comes to matters of the heart."

Nicholas caught a glimpse of moisture in Katherine's blue grey eyes, but she looked away as she continued speaking.

"I imagine that had I been alive in 1936, I would have been a big supporter of Edward and," she hesitated, "Wallis's." She smiled at Nicholas. "There, I've said her name. It would be wonderful to believe it was all about love, but the truth is much harsher and the only type of love these two 'royals' were capable of, was the utmost expression of self-love."

"So you're a romantic at heart?" Nicholas said, with a sly grin on his face.

"It may come as a surprise to you, but yes I am." She bristled in her seat and Nicholas sensed her irritation. "But these two plotted against Britain and committed treason. There is nothing romantic about that."

Nicholas waited while Katherine took a sip of water from her glass. "So you say all of this took place in 1941?"

"Correct."

"You mean it could have been over in 1941. The war could have been over?"

"Correct," she repeated. "I daresay, had their plan succeeded, Britain would have had no choice but to sue for peace and Edward would have returned as Hitler's puppet king."

Nicholas had heard these types of conspiracy theories before. "I know some people refer to Edward as the traitor king but these are just stories, fodder for the tabloids. I mean, here he was stuck out on an island somewhere in the middle of nowhere, how could he possibly have stirred up any trouble?"

"What … what are you smiling about?"

Katherine continued smiling.

"You look like the cat that ate the canary," he said, returning his cup to its saucer.

"The reason they almost got away with it was because of exactly that," she blurted out. "Who would have thought that they could get into any mischief in the Bahamas but, as fate would have it, and I hate to use such a cliché, Edward and Wallis landed smack dab in the middle of the future of the war when they arrived in Nassau in August 1940."

What did she mean, the future of the war?

"So, what exactly did they find when they got to Nassau?"

"Before I tell you the story," she began. "I first want to tell you that their Majesties plans were thwarted by the honor, courage, and dedication to country of one man and that man, who is unknown to history, saved the free world."

Nicholas realized that Katherine's tone had changed. What she was telling him was very real; at least it was to her.

"The great paradox is that this story, of courage and honor triumphing over treason and treachery, can never be told without revealing the best kept secrets of World War II." Katherine sat back up in her chair before continuing, "You see, to tell the truth and prove Edward's treachery, to resurrect the unknown hero who stopped Edward and Wallis would also reveal the greatest sins of Franklin Roosevelt and Winston Churchill. This would change history forever." Peering over her glasses at Nicholas, she continued, "Roosevelt was a man who had to choose between the lesser of two evils. He was able to do this by accepting his role as divinely assigned."

These were heavy words and Katherine delivered them with such gravity that Nicholas was momentarily stunned. "Divinely assigned," he mumbled. "What does that mean? I'm a little confused."

"You're confused because you have not grasped the true character of Franklin Roosevelt," Katherine said. "Roosevelt has been tagged as a traitor to his class because of his social programs and all of that, but the truth of the matter is that he was the closest thing to royalty that America ever produced. Oh, many people like to view John Kennedy and the Kennedy family as American royalty, but it was and always will be Franklin Roosevelt who ruled like royalty because he was cut from the same cloth as the royals."

"Are you saying that he was like a royal or he actually ruled as a King?"

"I am saying that Franklin Roosevelt understood the divine right of Kings and that to build an empire you needed to be as ruthless as a King; he just had to do it in a representative democracy, which made things a little more difficult."

Nicholas stayed silent for a few minutes.

"You're telling me that you have knowledge of some great sin or crime committed by Roosevelt and your justification for keeping that sin hidden is that Roosevelt was like a king? I don't understand you at all. Why would you protect this man who's not even British? And why would you assign him royal status?"

"Because he saved Britain," she replied, in a reverent whisper. "Because his decision, his great sin, saved the world and because the only way his original sin could be forgiven was by the grace of God himself."

Nicholas found himself exhaling as he looked at Katherine, "How do you know that this secret won't get out? Maybe it's already gotten out and it's no big deal."

Coming forward slowly in her chair and clearing her throat, "Oh these sins will never get out, not as long as I have breath in me, of that I am sure."

"There is more than one sin?

"Many more."

"How can you be so sure they won't come out? Nicholas said.

"Because I'm the only one who knows the secrets and I'm the only person who has the proof and these sins will remain hidden from the world as long as I am alive."

Nicholas stared at Katherine for a few moments. "But, you are going to tell me the story

"Yes, I am," replied Katherine.

"Why me?" He said, shrugging his shoulders. "Why are you telling me this story?"

Katherine rose from her seat and began walking about the room. Stopping at one of the large windows with her back to Nicholas, she asked, "what do you know about your father and his work?"

"Now you want to bring up my father," Nicholas said, running his fingers through his hair and slouching back into his chair. "I mean, you've just told me that you are in possession of some great secret, some big mystery and then, just like that, poof," he said, snapping his fingers. "You switch to my father?"

"The stories are connected," she replied. "Your father was molded by the same lessons of 1941 as I was and your father applied those lessons to his life and his work. History has a habit of repeating itself in all things, great and small." Turning around she faced Nicholas, "1941 shaped your father's actions in 1997 and for me to tell you about his life and his death, I need to tell you what happened in Nassau in 1941."

Nicholas took a moment before sitting back in his chair and nodding.

"Good," Katherine said, turning again to face the large window. "Now, I'll ask you again, what do you know about your father?"

"Not much," he replied. "My mother rarely speaks about him. I understand that he was some type of civil servant, but other than that I have no idea who he was or what he did."

Katherine spun on her heels and walked back towards Nicholas. Irritation flashed in her eyes.

"Your father was much more than a civil servant, and it pains me to have you dismiss him as such. He was a great man and a patriot. There are many people who would not agree with that assessment. Those people are sadly mistaken. Your father was a great man because he had the rare gift of being able to know what the right thing was and what to do about it."

Standing over Nicholas, she continued. "Your father, you see, served the crown in the most personal way and his sacrifice saved this country and the monarchy."

Nicholas was slightly taken aback with the more assertive manner in which Katherine bristled about his father being a simple civil servant, but he also found himself becoming angry.

"You seem to have a very high opinion of my father but I daresay, from my perspective, he was not that honorable a man. I mean this rare gift you say he had of knowing the right thing to do and doing it, didn't really apply to me now did it?"

Katherine backed away.

"You have every reason to be upset and hurt by the absence of your father in your life. And I know that he regretted the type of father circumstances and personal failings made him, but no man can be or should be judged on one aspect of their life."

"I probably agree with that for the most part," Nicholas said. "But I can't begin to tell you how much harder my life was without him. You see, my mother is a very weak woman, easily manipulated, and when she married Ratzenberger, well, my life became a living hell.

"My step father is a bully. An out and out bully; he bullies my mother and he bullied me until I left home. I had no one to protect me from him."

Nicholas rubbed both temples with his thumb and forefinger of his right hand before continuing.

"When I was younger, I would lie awake at night, especially after one of Ratzenberger's drunken tirades, in which he wielded his belt like a Samurai, and imagine my father coming to get me and take me out of there," he looked directly at Katherine before continuing. "But he never came and I eventually grew up and got the hell out of that house on my own accord."

Nicholas sat back, seemingly lost for a few moments.

Katherine's voice broke the silence. "I'm sorry that you went through those difficulties and I can understand, to a degree, the loss you feel. I lost my parents when I was ten years old. They were killed in a car accident, which is how I ended up being raised by my grandfather. I missed them terribly, but I did have the love and comfort of my grandfather and I had Franklyn to keep me company."

"I'm sorry about your parents," Nicholas replied, in a mumbled voice hoping she did not feel his sheepishness.

"And I'm sorry that you grew up without your father; I know that your father bore this same pain that you still bear today. It's odd," she said, a wry smile crossing her face, "You and your father were both victims of the same heartache."

Her smile faded into a light tear that formed in the corner of her right eye. Nicholas looked away. She had hit a nerve and he was doing everything in his power not to let the tears welling up behind his eyes show.

After a few minutes of sitting in silence, Nicholas said, "I don't want to seem rude or too forward, but what exactly was your relationship with my father?

"I loved your father," replied Katherine without hesitation. "And it is love that is at the heart of what I want to teach you."

"Are you going to teach me about my father or about love?" He said with a slight grin on his face.

'Love is a funny word," Katherine said. "I loved your father as a woman loves a man. Your father loved his country above all. I accepted that as not only, as it should be, but also as to who he was." Katherine shifted in her seat and looked directly at Nicholas. "There are men throughout history who have had the fortitude to do the most difficult of things in order for the greater good of mankind. These men go unheralded. There are no parades, no medals, and no accolades of any sort. The lucky ones go on to live quiet full lives, the greatest of all, well, they are always sacrificed in the service of what they loved. Your father was one of those men."

Nicholas sat transfixed. It was obvious that she had loved his father. Her eyes misted over every time she mentioned Andrew Stone and she spoke of him and his "service" with the utmost reverence. He felt odd that he was somehow comforted by the knowledge that his father was loved.

Katherine seemed to be in some sort of distant past as her words now flowed with an almost detached element to them.

"That yellow love seat, which so obviously doesn't fit in this room, belonged to your father. And the red

Spitfire in the picture that you were drawn to when you entered this room was your father's car." She paused before continuing. "I could never bring myself to part with either one."

Nicholas found himself trying to picture his father sitting on the love seat or down shifting the spitfire as he raced into a corner both images brought a smile to his face.

Katherine continued in her almost dream-like recitation. "Your father and I built a quiet life around his, shall we say, less than normal schedule, and around the fireplace in this very room. You see, your father was an intelligence officer in the service of the British government; a real life James Bond, if you will."

Those words were spoken in such a matter of fact manner that Nicholas had to repeat them to himself just to make sure he understood them.

He opened his mouth to speak, but no sound came out.

Katherine blinked her eyes a few times, as if to reset her thoughts. "We met at work. I was a low level administrator in the archive offices of British Intelligence. My grandfather had gotten me the position, as that was the line of work he was in and he knew everybody in the intelligence business. Your father came down to my section one day, to retrieve some information and…it was love at first sight."

A huge smile spread across Katherine's face and its infective nature caused Nicholas to smile in reaction.

"For both of us," she continued, getting up from her seat and walking toward the fireplace and taking a hold of the picture of the red Spitfire she said, "Your father loved this car. When you first walked into this room and you were immediately drawn to this picture." She paused and turned to face Nicholas. "It took my breath away. You are very much like your father and the fact that you love this car as much as he loved this car, well, it's a wonderful coincidence."

"Maybe it's more than that." Nicholas said. "Maybe it's in the genes?"

"That is what I have been banking on all along," Katherine said, a broad smile on her face.

Nicholas sat back contemplating her words. The picture of his father that was emerging was a far cry from what his mother had ever told him.

"I still have the Spitfire," Katherine said, turning to face Nicholas.

"What, you mean that same car?" Nicholas asked, pointing to the picture.

"Yes, that same car," Katherine replied. "I have kept it all of these years and I want you to have it. I have it out back in the garage."

Nicholas found himself unable to respond. It wasn't just the idea of a car that was overwhelming; it was that it was that car, his favorite car, and his father's car.

"I don't know what to say," he finally uttered.

"It's in good condition and I have kept it serviced and running," Katherine said. "It gives me such joy to see that you love it. It needs a new young owner."

Moments passed in silence.

"I would like to move on now," she said. "What did you think about Mr. Nash?" she asked.

"Nash?"

"Yes, Thomas Nash, the file I left you to read back in your classroom. What are your thoughts?"

Nicholas realized class was back in session.

"I liked him," he replied, re-engaging with Katherine. "He didn't take any crap from anyone and I think I can relate to that."

"Don't you feel that Nash was disloyal to his commanding officer?"

"I think he was loyal to his fellow soldiers over the buffoons who were in charge," Nicholas said.

"You mentioned that you could relate to Nash because he didn't take any 'crap,' as you put it, do you believe he was an honorable man?"

Nicholas thought for a moment before responding. "If you are asking me if it is honorable to stand up for what one believes then yes he had honor, but I don't know if he lived an honorable life by what little I know about him."

"Do you believe in an honorable death?" Katherine asked.

"I suppose so," he said, hesitating. "If it is in the service of something great or defending a loved one or an innocent from harm, I suppose a death can be honorable but I don't know if death itself is honorable."

Katherine rose from her chair and made her way to the other side of the room. A small end table with a solitary lamp on it stood in the corner of the room. She retrieved a file and handed it to Nicholas.

"I would like you to read through this file," she said. "I need to check on Franklyn who is preparing dinner. I'm sure a young man like you has a healthy appetite so let's get you fed; you have a lot of reading to do and we have a long night ahead of us."

With those words, Katherine rose from her seat and kissed the top of Nicholas's forehead before leaving the room.

The unexpected display of affection somehow comforted him as he sat staring at the new file she had placed in front of him. He felt an overwhelming need to know all that this woman knew about his father.

He sat up in his seat and opened the file Katherine had placed in front of him. The label read:

ROLPH WIEGARD - NASSAU BAHAMAS -1941

CHAPTER FOUR

"Where does his majesty believe you are this afternoon?" Rolf Wiegard asked over his shoulder, as he stood staring out at the water from the large bay window of his bedroom.

"What, what are you asking me?" came the reply from deep within the covers of his oversized canopy bed.

"His majesty, Edward, your husband," Wiegard said, turning around to face the Duchess of Windsor. "Where did you tell your husband you were going this afternoon?"

He looked directly at the half-naked Wallis and couldn't help but wonder how such a small woman could have such an inexhaustible appetite for sex.

"I told him I was touring the eastern end of the island with some of the society ladies, looking for rare tropical plants or something to that effect," she said, waving her hands as if to dismiss the question. "Why, do you fear my husband?" she continued, gathering the covers around her.

Rolf Wiegard smiled and approached the side of the bed. "Tell me my dear, why do you do it?"

"Do what?" she replied.

"Why do you sleep with other men? Does his Majesty not suffice?" he asked sitting down on the bed.

"I'm not sure I understand your question," she hesitated. "I feel you are attempting to embarrass me."

"Not at all," he replied. "I'm just trying to understand you. For me, I will be honest; I get a perverse sense of satisfaction in bedding another man's wife. I was just curious as to why you do it."

"Is that it then, Rolf? She asked. "Is that it? Am I just another man's wife for you to bed?"

"You play games with me, my dear. I was just asking a simple question." Rising from the bed, he walked over to the desk and lit a cigarette.

"I suppose I do it out of boredom," Wallis said, as she sat up in the bed. "Life here on this island is dreadful. You, Rolf, you, are my entertainment."

Wiegard smiled to himself as he drew on his cigarette. "I love this island. For sailing and fishing, this is the place to be. I don't share your dismay for the life here in these waters."

"That's because you like sailing and fishing and because you are a freak of nature," she said, taking a cigarette from the nightstand.

Wiegard picked up a silver plated lighter from the desk and bent over the bed as Wallis held her head up giving him the tip of her cigarette to light.

Sitting back into the pillows and inhaling the tobacco, Wallis continued. "You are Swiss yet you are almost as dark as some of the natives in these islands. If it weren't for you greasing you black hair down, well," she exhaled a thin stream of smoke and looked directly at him, "People might mistake you for one of the natives."

His left eye twitched first, and Wiegard felt the irritation rise in him. This shrew had the temerity to place herself above him in some racial purity pecking order and he felt the anger begin to rise.

"You are also free to travel on business to Miami, Washington and New York at will," she continued, speaking almost to herself. "I, on the other hand am banished to this place because of my brother-in-law, the King, and that bastard Churchill."

"Respectfully, my dear," He began, making a great effort to calm himself. "Your country or rather Edward's country, is at war with Germany and you and your husband were not very accommodating to Mr. Churchill or your brother-in-law, the King."

"You overthink these things, Rolf," she said forcefully stumping out her cigarette in the ashtray. "My brother-in-law, stuttering fool that he is, and his dowdy wife could not and cannot hold a candle to Edward and me. This banishment is designed to humiliate and punish us for being more loved by the people than they are."

Wiegard smiled to himself. This wretched woman was under the illusion that she was beloved by the British people, when in actuality; they loved Edward and despised her for taking him away.

"I have been living here on and off for over fifteen years," Wiegard said, as he rose and walked back toward the large bay window. "It is the perfect place for me to be based out of to deal with the Americans. Besides," he said spreading his arms out wide, "look how magnificently beautiful the water is. I could no more live back home after experiencing this paradise."

"But Switzerland is where your factories are as well as where your wife and children reside, may I remind you," Wallis said. "Have you forgotten about her and your two daughters, isolated from the world as we are here?"

"The factories are in Switzerland," he began, ignoring her sarcasm. "But the market for my technologies is the U.S., and specifically the American military. Further still, there are some pesky South American strongmen that are also good-paying customers. That is why I have based myself out of Nassau. It's easier to do business with the Americas from here."

"You and your business talk," she said, as she ruffled the pillows around her head. "We are hosting a dinner for your Colonel Wilkerson this very evening and I have no idea how any of it helps your business."

"Why, my dear," he said turning around to face her. "You underestimate your star power. You and Edward are still very glamorous people, especially to those simple-minded Americans. Wilkerson has just concluded a large purchase of my hydraulic technology for the American Navy, and meeting you and His Majesty will give him a lifetime of stories to tell to his wife and friends back home."

"Humph," Wallis replied. "I can't tell if you are mocking me or if you are sincere."

"Oh I am always sincere," he said as he walked back to the large bay window and marveled at the ever-changing turquois blue waters before him.

Rolf Wiegard wondered if the cuckolded Edward had told Wallis about his true reason for being in Nassau. After all, she was the man's wife. Wiegard had easily manipulated Edward into his schemes as soon as the royal couple was in residence. The promise of a return to power and glory was too sweet an enticement for Edward to resist. Wiegard needed the Governor General of the Island to do some of the things that only

Government could do, Edward had become a major part of Wiegard's plans.

He could hear Wallis's voice droning on behind him and he felt the irritation rise in him again. Her earlier mocking of his dark coloring and all that it implied flashed through his mind. Turning back toward the bed, he undid the chord of his robe and let the garment drop to the floor. He saw the realization flash across her eyes and she instantly knew his intent. He wanted her one more time before the evening's festivities. He needed to hurt her and he knew exactly what he wanted to do.

"No, Rolf," she began in protest. "I have to get back to Government House. We are after all hosting Colonel Wilkerson in just a couple of hours."

"This won't take long, my dear," he said with a snarl, as he mounted the bed and grabbed hold of the back of her head. "Turn over; this is all I want to think about tonight while I am dining with your husband."

CHAPTER FIVE

June 5th, 2013
Katherine Blackwood's Sitting Room

Nicholas felt Katherine's presence as she slipped back into the room. He had closed his eyes and put his head back against the deep padded chair-back.

"Am I disturbing your nap?" she asked as she approached his seat.

"Who wrote this?" Nicholas countered without opening his eyes.

"Why do you ask?" replied Katherine.

"It's written as a story as a narrative. So was the file you gave me about Thomas Nash. This was written by someone who was there," he opened his eyes and sat up. "Who wrote this and why am I being told stories?"

Katherine sat down on the sofa opposite Nicholas and waited a moment before speaking.

"I told you that your father was one of those people who had the capacity to do the unthinkable and to go unrecognized in history for the greatness of their sacrifice. I knew another such man, before I ever met your father, and I loved him too.

He also was a man capable of doing the inconceivable, in the greater service of good. I learned from both him and your father the true meaning of honor. This man, you see, was my grandfather, Oliver Blackwood."

She removed her glasses with her left hand before continuing, "What you are reading are his words, his accounting of what transpired and I assure that what you are reading is authentic and what you are learning is real."

"May I ask what your objective is? Why are you giving me pieces of a story?"

"I have told you already, I'm teaching you."

She waited a moment before continuing.

"My grandfather painstakingly documented, almost down to the moment, acts of treachery and bravery and the ultimate act of honor. He was uniquely placed in this saga, and that is what it was, a saga. He was witness to and had influence in almost every aspect of the story."

Katherine paused and produced a white handkerchief, which she used to clean her eyeglasses. "He interviewed everybody involved ad nauseam. Knowing him and the way he was, it was probably more of an inquisition or deposition than an interview. He could be quite harsh and he was always the smartest person in the room, always three steps ahead of you. He documented everything. Every thought, every emotion, every recollection and he collected everything: secret memos, ship logs, personal papers, highly secret reports, banking records and even transcripts of telephone conversations."

She put her glasses back on before continuing, "he was an eyewitness to a secret history and he amassed an archive of confidential material including a letter in Roosevelt's own hand that in and of itself, would shock the world and change history forever."

Nicholas sat captivated by her words. He had just been introduced to the mysterious Rolf Wiegard and he could sense the building up of the story as Katherine revealed it but now she was telling him that this strange and unraveling tale had a paper trail.

He loosened his tie, as it had grown warm in the room. "It all sounds so nefarious, but why would your grandfather go to such lengths to document something only to keep it hidden?"

"Nothing stays hidden forever," Katherine said as she took her seat opposite Nicholas. "If there is one thing history has taught us, it's that all is revealed in due time."

Nicholas thought about her words and started to speak, but caught himself. If this tale is as earth shattering as she had implied and if there was proof in her grandfather's files, then Katherine was sitting on a bombshell of a story.

"I know that the truth has to come out," Katherine said. "I believe my grandfather knew this too. They say confession is good for the soul.

"Everyone who matters will be dead when the story comes out."

"But you, ah, said these great sins would never come out as long as…"

"As long as I am alive," she said, interrupting Nicholas. "I'm not going to live forever and when you confess these men, I won't be around to see it."

"I'm not sure I understand," he asked. "What do you mean, confess these men?"

"You, Nicholas, you," she said, sitting up in her chair. "You are going to be the one to tell their story but mind you. You won't have a single shred of evidence that proves anything unless I feel you have learned the lessons that I need to teach you."

Nicholas bristled in his chair. "I'm confused as to exactly what it is that you want to teach me, could you be more specific?" he asked.

"I realize we come from two different sides of the social equation. And that we probably disagree on most political and social matters, but we are both British and that should unite us."

Folding her hands in her lap, she continued. "It is my intent to teach you about honor and sacrifice; service to the crown. To tell you not only who and what your father was but also how he died." Pointing both index fingers at Nicholas and raising her voice she said, "There are plenty of sins to go around here. Roosevelt's, Churchill's, my grandfather's, and your father's, for all of that to come out, well it would have to be delivered by someone who believed that what these men did was necessary although," she paused, lowering her hands back to her lap, "morally indefensible."

Nicholas sat silent for a few moments absorbing what Katherine had just said and he measured his words carefully before asking, "I don't mean to be rude or anything, but don't you have any children or other relatives who might want to continue-"

"Continue what?" she said, interrupting. "Have another person live a life of silent desperation? It is a terrible thing to live your life with secrets and I wouldn't want that for anyone. Besides," she said, as a look of sadness crossed her face, "I am the last of my line; I have no children and no family save for Franklyn."

The coughing came on suddenly and violently.

Katherine quickly produced some tissue and covered her mouth but not before Nicholas saw a sliver of blood on the corner of her lip.

"Please excuse me," she said, her voice coarser. "I need a few moments, Continue reading and I will be with you shortly."

Nicholas rose from his seat as Katherine left the room. He could hear her coughing begin again as she closed the door behind her.

She was ill, gravely ill. She had coughed up blood. The realization jolted him to his feet and he found himself facing the picture of the red Triumph Spitfire, his father's car.

It was all too much and he was craving a drink. Katherine was revealing some great secret to him from 1941, and somehow it related to the truth about his father, but she was sick and he felt an overwhelming sense of melancholy that he didn't quite understand.

As he continued to stare at the Spitfire, Nicholas's mind began to wonder. He could see his father and Katherine motoring down some side country road. Her hair, tied with a scarf because the top would be down. That would fit the image that he was developing about his father.

Katherine coughing up blood flashed into his mind and broke his trance with the Spitfire. He walked to the small bar that was to the left of the double oak doors. The bar was stocked with half-filled bottles of rum, gin and scotch, along with several glass tumblers that sat polished on top of a silver tray.

Nicholas opened the scotch and poured a glass. He replaced the bottle and took the tumbler back to the armchair and sat down. The file on Rolf Wiegard lay open where he had stopped reading. Raising the tumbler of scotch toward the picture of his father's car,

Nicholas toasted his memory and swallowed the contents of the glass.

Putting the glass down firmly on the table, he picked up the file and continued reading.

CHAPTER SIX

Sunday, July 20th, 1941
8 p.m.
Government House
Nassau, Bahamas

Rolf Wiegard watched from the front portico of Government house as Colonel Adam T. Wilkerson climbed the steps from Duke Street up to where he stood. It was 8 p.m., and as his military training dictated, the Colonel was right on schedule.

It didn't surprise Wiegard that the man wore his American Army Officer uniform; he was unable to conceal his excitement when Wiegard extended an invitation on behalf of their majesties for cocktails at Government house.

"Good of you to be on time," Wiegard said, extending his right hand towards Colonel Wilkerson, as he reached the front Portico of the house.

"I really appreciate the invite. My wife isn't going to believe me when I get back to Maryland, I mean," he said, lowering his eyes. "We're originally from a small town in Kansas ... Nobody back home could ever imagine meeting a real live king, even though I know he is no longer the king."

Wiegard smiled, allowing the colonel to ramble. These Americans were so easy to impress, he thought. No wonder his handlers were not concerned with them.

The Colonel, despite his whimsical youth, was a senior procurement officer with the United States Armed Services and had come to Nassau to finalize the purchase of several million dollars of Wiegard's hydraulic technologies.

In addition to the generous cash bonus he had paid the Colonel, Wiegard had arranged the cocktail reception. He had one smaller piece of business to conduct with the young Colonel before the American returned to Washington and tonight was the perfect opportunity to ask.

"Never offer your hand to his majesty," Wiegard said, extending his arm out motioning the Colonel to enter the residence. "He does not like to touch people or for people to touch him."

"Okay," Wilkerson replied with a stammer. "Maybe I'll just salute him."

Wiegard smirked to himself. That was exactly what Edward craved. This young American officer saluting him would feed Edward's ego and make the evening that much more pleasant.

Leading the Colonel into the large foyer of Government House, Wiegard looked back at him. "Her ladyship is originally from Baltimore, so you two will have something in common."

"I guess," Wilkerson replied, as his eyes scanned the oil paintings that decorated the mansion's walls.

"This way," Wiegard said. "I believe their majesties are already out on the terrace."

The east terrace of Government House was a large stone covered patio with a collection of whicker and stone chairs scattered about. Edward and Wallis along with another couple were engaged in light chatter as two butlers stood by ready to meet any and all demands.

Wallis was the first to spot the new arrivals. "Look my dear," she said, tugging at Edward's sleeve. "Rolf and his guest have arrived."

Edward turned toward the arriving guests. Squaring his stance, he folded his arms behind his back and waited to be introduced.

Wiegard had witnessed this ritual before and tried to hide his smile. Edward insisted on always having guests presented to him as if he still reigned over some medieval court.

"Your Royal Highness," Wiegard said, bowing ever so slightly. "May I present Colonel Adam Wilkerson of the United States Armed Services?"

Wiegard had barely finished his introduction when Wilkerson snapped to attention and saluted Edward.

"Your majesty, it is my great honor to meet you."

Edward nodded ever so slightly.

"And this is her Ladyship, the Duchess of Windsor," Wiegard said, extending his hand towards Wallis. The earlier events of the day flashed through his mind. Not a hair out of place and her makeup was perfect, and he had so ravaged her just a few hours earlier.

"Ma'am," Wilkerson said, turning toward Wallis and removing his cap.

"Colonel Wilkerson," Wallis said, extending her right hand to the American. "Welcome to Government House."

Wilkerson fumbled, took Wallis' hand, bent over and kissed it. "Thank you for having me."

Taking her hand back and casting a glance toward Wiegard, Wallis said. "It is our pleasure to host you this evening. Mr. Wiegard tells me you live in Baltimore, is that correct?"

"It is, ma'am, but I am originally from a small town in Kansas."

"Kansas," Wallis began with a laugh, "We are a long way from Kansas but you know I'm originally from Baltimore. I wonder if we know any of the same people."

Without waiting for a reply, Wallis turned toward the couple standing behind Edward, "These are our dear friends, Commissioner David Atkinson and his wife Nancy. The Commissioner is in charge of the police and Nancy, well Nancy is just the dearest person you will ever meet."

As the Atkinsons and the royal couple exchanged pleasantries with the American Colonel, Wiegard lit a cigarette and accepted a glass of champagne from one of the butlers. He walked over to the far side of the terrace and fixed his gaze towards Hog Island, which, at this hour of the evening, could only be seen as a dark shadow in the distance.

Hog Island laid a half-mile east of the northern shore of Nassau Town. It got its name because for years that was where the locals kept their hogs. It had a natural harbour on the northeast side and an extensive network of natural caves.

Wiegard congratulated himself as he thought of what he had secretly built on that island. He had manipulated Edward into relocating the few residents of Hog Island so that there were no pesky locals about to interfere with his plans.

Edward had been easily seduced. Wiegard had wasted very little time in sitting Edward down and telling him whom he really served. Edward's reaction was at first almost comical, as his jaw dropped in amazement and he was able to mumble his utter disbelief that Herr Hitler had such an operation right under the nose of the British Government and in America's backyard.

From that moment on, Edward became a pawn in Wiegard's hands. The promise of once again reigning as sovereign over the British people, even under the tutelage of Adolph Hitler, was too much for the lusty Edward to resist.

Hog Island and its network of caves and natural harbour was the perfect location for the secret laboratory that Wiegard had built and was now operating at full capacity. This laboratory was now building the weapon that would win the war.

He had spared no expense in outfitting the caves and constructing a support building to the exact specifications that the German engineers and scientists, who now labored there nonstop, had asked for.

He had built housing for these German scientists and had used laborers from South America to construct what was needed. Once the work was completed, the workers were sent back. Unfortunately, their ship exploded and sank and never made it home.

The fate of the Venezuelan workers was never far from Wiegard's mind. Tonight his plan was to enlist the help of Colonel Wilkerson in making some security arrangements independent of his Nazi handlers.

Wiegard finished his cigarette and turned back towards the gathered group in time to hear Edward say to Commissioner Atkinson, "Our understanding is that you had a little excitement in court this morning, is that correct Commissioner?"

"Well, as you know, sir, some of the locals we displaced from Hog Island filed court papers claiming they were harmed by your decision to vacate the island. The court ruled in your graces favor this afternoon and the plaintiffs were just acting out," the Commissioner said. "Nothing extraordinary, sir."

Wiegard examined the Commissioner's face carefully. He didn't quite believe that the man was easily fooled. He had not taken kindly to being told that even he was not allowed to go to Hog Island.

Edward turned toward Wiegard. "This is precisely of what we were speaking of just the other day. One cannot expect these locals to understand progress. They are worried about their little spot of land and cannot see past the end of their noses."

"They are a simple people," The Commissioner began. "And one cannot expect them to have the foresight of our Mr. Wiegard here. I have tried to assure them that whatever Mr. Wiegard is doing on Hog Island will have long term economic benefits for them."

Wiegard smiled. "My dear Commissioner, what I am doing on Hog Island will have long term and very consequential benefits to the history and economy of this little colony."

The irony of this statement was for him alone to enjoy.

Wiegard felt the need to placate the Commissioner. No need to poke a potential adversary in the eye, unless one was set on picking a fight.

"I know that my heavy handed approach towards Hog Island has not set well with you, Commissioner, but please understand it is out of the utmost respect for your position and your person that I insisted His Majesty bar everyone, including you, from Hog Island."

The backhanded compliment seemed to have its effect as the Commissioner started to respond before Wiegard cut him off.

"I meant no disrespect to you personally it's just that in my line of work, we sometimes experiment with chemicals and things that go 'boom'! I thought it best to protect everyone."

A light chorus of laughter from the gathered responded to Wiegard's emphasizing the word boom.

As the Commissioner replied that there were no hard feelings, Wiegard's mind drifted to what was going on the northeast side of Hog Island at this very moment. The moonless night and the stillness of the air gave the perfect cover for the German U- boat that had surfaced fifty yards offshore.

German efficiency, he thought to himself. They would have the last of the equipment and supplies unloaded and on their way before the sun broke the darkness. Wiegard suspected that the fate of the German scientists now on Hog Island would be the same as the Venezuelan construction workers. He had been assured that these scientists had sworn an oath of loyalty to Hitler himself, but his instinct told him otherwise.

Tonight, he would ask Colonel Wilkerson to recommend a bodyguard. A buffer was needed between him and his German handlers. After all, as elite as he felt he was and as valuable as the work that he was doing was, he knew the German regime was ruthless.

He knew that he was as expendable as the common foot soldier.

"The war is going well for Germany eh?" Edward asked Wiegard.

"It seems that way, sir. As we have discussed many times, the superior power will eventually win out and the Aryan is the superior power."

"You are quite right," Edward replied. "Just look at this damn place," he gestured to the horizon. "These locals would still be sucking on coconuts had we not shown them the civilized world. Their culture is supposedly older than our culture so how do you justify their lack of progress?"

Wiegard began to respond but Edward cut him off.

"They are an inferior race!" Edward announced, taking a drink from the silver tray being held by one of the black butlers. "It's not their fault that they were born to the Negro race; it's just their great misfortune. This is why our country will lose this war because we allowed Britain to become overrun with lesser people. France has crumbled because she was internally diseased and we fear Britain will follow."

Wiegard marveled at Edward's ability to ignore the black servant standing next to him. His Majesty's Aryan soul was never more on display than when he did not acknowledge the existence of those who served him.

"Now, now," Wallis said. "The evening has just begun and is quite young, let's not get all worked up."

"I say, old man." Edward's tone changed dramatically. "Wallis has hit on a splendid idea that will really lift the spirits of everyone and infuse our little colony with some much needed excitement."

Wallis had gotten up from her seat and was now standing next to Edward and had taken his hand as he continued to say, "We have decided to ask our brother, the King, to send their Royal Highness's Elizabeth and Margaret to winter with their old uncle in the Bahamas. We have decided to invite the Royal Princesses to Christmas with us this year."

Wiegard hoped his surprise didn't show. "That sounds like a wonderful plan, your Majesty. We must make certain that we have a lot of activities planned for the young ladies."

The other gathered guests, including Colonel Wilkerson, all joined in with their approval and congratulations. Wiegard tried to catch Wallis's eye as his sixth senses told him there was more to this story.

This little visit that Wallis had dreamed up could not be more ill timed for his plans. Christmas 1941 was the deadline that Berlin had set for his grand experiment to be launched; this was just another wrinkle to deal with.

Nancy Atkinson had gone into the main house to use the facilities and Wallis started looking around for her. "I believe Nancy has gone inside and I am a bit hungry, why don't we all go in and have some dinner?"

"Splendid, my love," Edward replied, lighting a cigarette. "One more smoke and then we'll come in."

"Very well," replied Wallis. "Come Rolf," she said taking Wiegard's arm. "Escort me in, if you please."

Taking Wallis's hand Wiegard started toward the screen doors leading back into the house. "I must say my dear, you are full of surprises."

"You have no idea," Wallis replied in a stern voice. "I am not the type of person to just lie down; I have my own plans to return my idiot husband to the throne."

Wiegard thought this statement to be odd and out of context. "I wish you had spoken with me before you made your plans."

"Oh, am I required to ask your approval?" she replied, her voice rising in sarcasm. "I don't answer to his majesty; don't believe for one minute that I will answer to you."

"I didn't mean that," Wiegard said feeling the irritation in him rise. "Your timing is just off. That was all that I wanted to say."

"My timing is perfect. And my plans don't require your approval." She stopped and turned to him, a sly smile appeared across her face. "When the princesses arrive, you are going to kidnap them."

With that, she spun on her heel and led the way into the dining room.

Wiegard stood for a moment, stunned by Wallis's latest scheme. It wasn't the first time that he had been shocked by Wallis and now he was sure that Edward had told her everything.

He spotted Nancy Atkinson standing a few feet away, looking ill at ease. Wiegard's stomach lurched. Had she heard their conversation? He smiled at her, attempting to appear as if he and Wallis had been discussing nothing more than the weather.

Nancy Atkinson quickly composed herself and gave him a curt smile before following Wallis into the dining room.

Wiegard trailed behind her, unable to shake the feeling that Wallis had just exposed everything.

CHAPTER SEVEN

June 5th, 2013
Katherine Blackwood's Sitting Room

Nicholas sat dumbfounded, his mind racing. He had remembered his history and he knew that Edward had been sent to the Bahamas as Governor General in 1940. He had heard the rumors and whispers about Edward's Nazi sympathies but had not really given them much credence. Like most people, he thought Edward to be nothing more than a star-crossed lover who gave up the throne as a grand gesture to love and romance.

Now, Katherine was revealing a Machiavellian side to Edward and a story that indicted him in a conspiracy of treason and treachery.

"Are you all right?" Katherine asked, observing Nicholas's bewilderment.

"Yes, I'm fine," he replied. "I'm just trying to get my thoughts around it all and I 'm not sure where to begin. I mean, I never heard of this Wiegard character and obviously the royal princesses were never kidnapped, so I'm a bit confused."

"Oh, but you do know of Wiegard's company," she replied. "He is obviously no longer amongst the living, but the company he built is still in business and still a major conglomerate with all sorts of defense and armament capabilities and contracts."

Nicholas rubbed his forehead. "Are you saying that the Duke of Windsor, along with his wife were involved in an attempt to kidnap the royal princesses and somehow they were also involved with the development of some type of weapon that Germany was building in the Bahamas?"

"Correct."

"Edward and Wallis conspired with a Swiss industrialist named Wiegard, to one, build a weapon for war, and two, to kidnap the royal Princesses. That is what you are saying," he repeated.

"At the risk of sounding redundant, yes."

"But neither event happened," continued Nicholas. "So I am still confused."

"The princesses were never kidnapped, but the weapon was built," Katherine said. "And Edward was complicit in both the kidnapping plans and the development of the weapon. You will understand more as I continue to reveal what occurred."

They both sat in silence for a few minutes and Nicholas realized that Katherine was giving him time to digest it all. He found his thoughts split between the great mystery about what happened in Nassau in 1941, and Katherine's illness.

"So, what happened next?" he asked.

"Well, first things first," she answered. "Are you hungry?'

Nicholas looked at his watch. It was twenty minutes past 8.

"I am a bit hungry," he said.

"Good. Franklyn left some cold chicken in the icebox and a fresh summer salad. Let's go into the kitchen and get a bite to eat and let me tell you a little bit more about my Grandfather, Oliver Blackwood." Katherine rose from her seat and headed out to the kitchen area.

Nicholas got up and followed her wondering what else she had in store.

CHAPTER EIGHT

Sunday, August 10th, 1941
4 a.m.
No. 10 Downing Street

Oliver Blackwood waited patiently outside the entrance to Winston Churchill's private office. He thought back to the last time he was in these same offices and the decision his lifelong friend, the Prime Minister, had made that day.

A mere two months after Churchill took office, he ordered the sinking of the French fleet. Oliver Blackwood was the person most responsible for influencing Churchill's decision, and he was unofficial, retired, and completely off the record.

The act was met with international condemnation but Churchill and Blackwood were under no illusions as to how difficult it would be to defeat the Germans.

After all, this was war.

Blackwood smiled reluctantly to himself as he recounted his analysis. His greatest fear was that Britain did not have enough leaders who were ruthless enough to wage war with Hitler.

Germany had signed an armistice with France, after bringing the French to their knees. Churchill, at the behest of all of his war cabinet, pleaded with French Admiral Francois Darlan to scuttle his ships, sail them to America or join with the English Navy.

One thing was for certain; Nazi Germany would not be allowed to gain control over the French fleet.

French Admiral Darlan gave Churchill assurances that the fleet would not come under German control. But Oliver Blackwood knew better. Blackwood was the sole voice that stood for destroying the allied French fleet. He had learned from the last Great War that he would rather have a division of German troops in front of him than a division of French troops behind him.

The most powerful concentration of French war ships was the fleet that was docked in the port of Mers-el-Kebir in French Algeria. Churchill had already ordered the British Navy to the area ans issued the French an ultimatum. As negotiations dragged on, he ordered the attack, decimating the French fleet and killing over 1,200 French sailors.

That night Winston Churchill learned that the only person other than himself, brutal enough to take on Hitler was Oliver Blackwood, and he was not even a member of Government.

The door to Churchill's office opened and a young stenographer slipped out.

"You may go in now, sir," she said.

He thanked her, noticing how young she looked. Blackwood found it fitting that Churchill surrounded himself with young people. After all, his old friend had often been accused of being an overgrown adolescent. Entering the office, he quietly shut the door behind him.

Prime Minister Winston Churchill sat semi-reclined behind his desk, puffing on a large cigar staring straight up at the ceiling. Churchill's usually messy desk was bare except for a red folder, a bottle of scotch and two glasses, one empty and the other half drained of its contents.

Oliver Blackwood could not have resembled the Prime Minister less. He was tall -- about six feet, four inches with the taught athletic build of a long-distance runner. He was impeccably groomed and dressed in dark blue, pinstriped, double-breasted suite, a lavender tie and a gold tie clasp. Churchill, on the other hand, looked like a mess.

Blackwood could tell that his old school mate had not slept in some time.

"Good evening Prime Minister," Blackwood said.

"Good morning, Oliver," Churchill replied, grunting. "Come in, man. Come in."

Blackwood walked farther into the room and approached Churchill's desk. Rising from his desk, the Prime Minister walked around to greet his old friend. They shook hands and Churchill motioned to the sofas facing his desk.

"We have much to discuss this dark morning," Churchill said, walking over to the fireplace. He picked up a poker and stirred the ashes.

Blackwood sat in silence waiting.

Churchill stared into the fire, absent-mindedly rearranging the logs.

"I would not have asked you here at this hour unless it was for the most profound and disturbing of reasons, and yet I'm at a loss for words to express myself. Never thought you'd hear me say that now, eh?" Churchill continued, turning from the fire and smiling at Blackwood.

"These are trying times, Winston," Blackwood replied.

Churchill nodded in agreement and crossed back to his desk and filled both glasses with scotch.

Blackwood didn't normally drink, something that amazed Churchill. Blackwood argued that every drink was either a communion or a sentence, and he wished for neither.

Churchill sat down on the opposite sofa. "I am in possession of some disturbing information. What is even more disturbing is my decision as a consequence of this information." Churchill shifted in his seat. "I knew what I was getting into when I took this job, damn it Oliver, you know better than anyone that I wanted this job. I was put on this earth to do this job in this hour of history, but this decision I make with depravity in my soul as I choose to play God," lifting his eyes to meet Blackwood's, "a power granted only to a King."

Blackwood stared at him, and after a brief moment of silence, reached over, picked up the tumbler and took a swig of the Scotch.

"Now Winston," he began. "What is the nature of the information you have and what would lead you to such a dramatic decision?"

Churchill smiled at his friend before speaking. "There are people, some of them rather high up in our world, who do not wish us well in this great struggle we are involved with. I have often said that I did not become the King's first minister to preside over the destruction of his empire nor do I wish to preside over the destruction of the Monarchy itself."

Blackwood shifted in his seat and looked intently at the Prime Minister. Churchill stood up and once again moved to the fireplace. "I'm going to need another log in here," he said.

He stirred the ashes some more and walked around to the front of the desk. Gathering some papers, he put them into the red folder and handed them to Blackwood.

"Here, my friend. It's all in there. I can barely say the words that need to be said. I am asking you to commit treason with me because one of our own has committed treason against our people and our country and I will not allow it on my watch. In this case, two wrongs do make a right."

Oliver Blackwood knew immediately that his friend was serious. Churchill needed an 'off the grid', top secret, operation action in response to whatever it was that was in that red folder.

Blackwood picked up the file and after looking at Churchill for a long time.

"Winston," he said. "I have known you most of my life. I believe that you are the right person in the right place at precisely the right time. I have never had any reason to doubt your leadership and I won't begin now. We are in a struggle, my friend, one for our very existence. One in which I am not so naive as to believe that we will not have to, shall we say, break some eggs to get it done. Ask the French, but I am with you my friend. I have total faith in your judgment and I know we will win this war. Now, pour me another drink."

⇒⊱ ⊰⇐

Oliver Blackwood sat in the back seat of his car while his driver expertly maneuvered through London's dim streets. Dawn was breaking and his head was spinning.

Not since Mary Queen of Scots betrayed Queen Elizabeth had such an order been given. It wasn't breaking the law that bothered Blackwood; it was his sense of history that nagged at him. He knew that this decision and his actions would be judged if not today, then some day.

Blackwood had always doubted Edward, but Churchill, up until tonight, had been his biggest supporter. After abdication, Edward visited Nazi Germany in October of 1937 despite the British Government's advice against such a visit. Hitler received the Duke and the Duchess and during that visit, Edward gave the full Nazi salute while reviewing a squad of SS troops. The Duchess's sexual prowess was legendary amongst the intelligence officials. They were no stranger to the many liaisons and dalliances that she had with high-ranking German officials.

Tonight was the beginning of the end of this treachery.

Blackwood tapped his umbrella on the partition between him and his driver and addressed the man.

"James, we won't be going home just yet. Please make the next right turn you can."

The driver, glancing back through the rear view mirror and back at Blackwood, responded and turned at the next intersection. Blackwood sat back in his seat and cleared his thoughts: he knew exactly whom he needed for this job. Finding him was the easy part, convincing him to do Churchill's bidding would be quite another. Oliver Blackwood wished he hadn't had that second drink.

CHAPTER NINE

Friday, August 29th, 1941
2 p.m.
The Prince's Head Pub
Colchester, England

Thomas Nash noticed him as soon as he entered the pub. It was the suit that was out of place. This was a workingman's pub and one didn't see many suits in these parts.

He had settled into a routine in Colchester, but his instinct told himself that all that was about to change... the gentleman in the suit was going to have something to do with it.

Standing behind the bar wiping up an imaginary spot, Thomas kept his eye fixed on the second man who accompanied the older gentleman into the pub. This man was fit and in tip-top condition. The suite he wore did little to disguise his military training.

The younger man expertly scanned the entire pub and led the older gentleman to a seat at the bar.

Studying both men carefully, Thomas slid down the bar to where they had taken seats. "What can I get you fine gentlemen this afternoon?"

"Whiskey, neat," replied the older man, "And a glass of water for my driver, please."

Reaching under the bar for a bottle of whiskey, Thomas shifted his glance back to the driver. He poured out a shot of whiskey and placed it in front of the older man and then pouring out a glass of water and placing in front of the driver said, "We don't see too many fancy suites in this pub. You two seem a wee bit out of place."

The old man hadn't touched his drink and ignoring Thomas's remark, sat back in his bar stool and lit a cigarette. Taking several drags off the cigarette and exhaling slowly he locked eyes with Thomas before speaking.

"Tell me, Mr. Nash. Have you enjoyed your time off?"

Thomas stared at him, remaining silent. His mind was on full alert; this man knew his name.

"Your time here in this pub," continued the old man. "It's been a bit easier on you than the lads in the field, wouldn't you say?"

Thomas could feel the old man goading him and he felt his temper starting to flare.

"Who are you sir and what do you want?" he asked, leaning forward against the bar. "I've neither the patience nor inclination to play games."

"My name is Oliver Blackwood," the old man began, "Who I am is irrelevant. What I want is to give you your new orders."

Thomas, folding his arms, paused for a moment and then began to laugh.

"You must be mistaken, old man; I was discharged from His Majesty's Army. I don't take orders unless it's for a drink."

Blackwood smiled and continued to pull on his cigarette. The drinks remained, untouched.

"You Mr. Nash, are the one who is mistaken," Blackwood said. "You have never been discharged from the Army. In fact, you have been on leave and it's time for you to get back to work."

With that, Oliver Blackwood stubbed his cigarette out in an ashtray and pulled an envelope out of his jacket pocket, placing it on the bar. He stood up, took a one-pound note out of his wallet and laid it on the bar.

"In that envelope is all of the official paperwork you need to satisfy your curiosity. Take a look at it; you will find that it is all in order. You have ten days to report to the address in that envelope."

Without another word, Oliver Blackwood turned and walked out of The Princess's Head.

CHAPTER TEN

June 5th, 2013
Katherine Blackwood's kitchen

"I was wondering when we were going to get back to Thomas Nash," Nicholas said, handing his empty dish to Katherine who had donned a kitchen apron and was washing up. "He was after all the first person you introduced me to, the first file you gave me to read."

Katherine smiled. "There are a couple of heroes in this story and Thomas Nash is one. In fact he was the main one, the one who goes unheralded." Her voice trailed off and Nicholas felt that same sense of sadness emanate from her as when she talked about his father.

"And your grandfather," Nicholas said. "He seems like a character from an old movie, somewhat mysterious."

Katherine smiled again. "Oh he was no mystery; he was probably the most pragmatic, realistic man I have ever known, quite ruthless if the truth be told and dedicated to his country."

"You say he was retired, yet he seems to be at the center of this story," Nicholas said.

"Churchill and my grandfather were both in their sixties," Katherine said. " Old school mates, both still full of piss and vinegar, as if they were seventeen, both feisty and combative in defending their principals, but my grandfather preferred to operate in the shadows rather than in the open like the Prime Minister. Once you are in the intelligence business, there is no retirement."

Nicholas leaned up against the kitchen counter, lost in his thoughts; Katherine finished putting the dishes away.

Turning to him she asked, "Did you enjoy your meal?"

"I did. I didn't realize how hungry I was and I thank you."

"Don't thank me," She continued. "Thank Franklyn -- he knows his way around the kitchen."

"He seems very dedicated to you."

"He is," Katherine replied, wiping her hands on a dishtowel. "And he has been a great comfort to me over the years, especially when I first came to this house as a ten year old girl."

"So how did Franklyn come to be a member of your grandfather's household? Nicholas asked.

"He arrived in 1942 at the age of seventeen," she replied. "My grandfather chose to save his life, and he has been here ever since."

Locking eyes with Nicholas she said, "Franklyn is also a hero in this story. Fate has placed him in the middle and if there is any redemption for my grandfather to be had, it lies in the fact that Franklyn Gibson lives and has lived a full and storied life."

Nicholas had a hundred questions on the tip of his tongue, but Katherine quickly changed tone and said, "Now, let us retire to the sitting room and I will continue, unless of course you are tired and we can continue another day."

"No, no, of course not," he replied. "You definitely have my attention and curiosity so I'm not going anywhere until you kick me out."

He knew there was more to Franklyn's story, but he was beginning to understand that Katherine was leading him slowly to some pre-determined conclusion.

"Good," she replied, leading the way back to her sitting room. "Let us continue."

CHAPTER ELEVEN

Saturday August 30th, 1941
9:00 AM
Nassau Harbour

Rolf Wiegard sat in the back seat of his car writing furiously in his personal journal. It was a habit that he had developed from childhood and the daily, almost hourly recordings of his life were all kept in leather binders that he stored in his private office on the first floor of his residence. He had found this habit useful in recalling meetings and conversations both with business people as well as personal relationships, often wondering if he ever wrote his life story how useful these journals would be.

The car was pulled over to the side of the road opposite the dock where the Steamer from New York was just tying up. His driver stood outside the car absentmindedly polishing the hood with old worn cheesecloth. On the seat next to him was the file that contained all of the information on Manfred Krueger.

He had studied it for hours.

Wiegard placed the journal and Krueger's file in his briefcase and climbed out of the car. He made his way to the ship, eager to see if he could spot the young man he had hired among the disembarking passengers.

It pleased Wiegard that the 29-year-old Manfred Krueger was of German descent. He had grown up in a suburb of Chicago, but both parents had been born in Germany.

He went by Manny in school; Wiegard attributed this to his youth and trying to fit into American society. He was a star athlete in high school and fluent in both English and German.

Wiegard wanted a "buffer" between himself and Berlin and he calculated that bringing in an "enforcer" outside of Berlin's control would somehow offer him a level of protection. He believed in Berlin, he wanted a seat at the table but he knew better than to trust them. Covering his bets was his best move and Colonel Wilkerson had assured him that Manfred Krueger was that buffer.

It wasn't just the Nazis who Wiegard was growing wary of. It was also Wallis. Things had calmed down but she was still insisting on carrying through with her plans for the Royal Princesses. Wiegard had hoped by avoiding the topic, it would somehow go away but he knew better. Wallis was not one to let things sit for very long and inevitably she would return to the subject.

Wiegard scanned the crowd. As usual, the locals were pestering the passengers, offering them porter and tour-guide services, as well as local coconut drinks and delicacies soaked in a bit of rum.

He was examining some faces milling about on the dock when a voice from behind startled him.

"Mr. Wiegard?"

He spun around and came face to face with a young man who was about the same height as he, but with a much slimmer build. The young man's jet-black hair and dark grey eyes threw him off. He had been expecting a fairer, Aryan type given Krueger's heritage.

Perhaps, it wasn't Krueger. He wished now that he had asked the colonel for a photograph.

"Excuse me, sir," continued the young man. "You are Mr. Wiegard, right?"

"I am," he replied. "And you are...?

The man set his case on the ground and extended his right hand. "Manfred Krueger at your service. It's a pleasure meeting you, sir. I'm looking forward to working for you."

Krueger had an infectious smile, and Wiegard found himself smiling back as he accepted the young man's hand. "Yes, well … very nice to meet you, too, Mr. Krueger. I trust you had an uneventful journey?"

"Everything was great," replied Krueger. "I really enjoy being out at sea."

Wiegard found himself a little put off by Krueger's youthful exuberance. A pang of doubt in his gut had him second-guessing his decision. Maybe he had just gotten used to the dour German guards and scientists on Hog Island, but Krueger's enthusiasm was somehow unsettling.

For all intents and purposes, Krueger was immensely qualified for the position, having joined the U.S. Army right out of high school and having graduated from the elite American School of Special Operations.

The file detailed some of Krueger's accomplishments: expert shot, top of his class, highly trained in both hand-to-hand combat and explosives. Not to mention the Krueger family's political leanings. His father was decidedly pro-German and even harbored thoughts about returning the family to Germany.

Wiegard did his best to dismiss his reservations and gestured toward his car. "Come, my car is right this way. We have a lot to talk about."

"Ready, willing and able." Krueger reclaimed his case and followed Wiegard away from the dock.

They drove out of Nassau Harbour and made their way west on Bay Street. This was the drive to Wiegard's personal residence and he wanted to take the time to get a better understanding of this man Krueger. The road, narrow at times, was lined on either side with tall pine trees, which had the effect of partially blocking out the sun. Light beams danced off of the polished hood. Openings in the road popped up every 300 of 400 feet, leading to dirt paths – and eventually to the water.

Scattered intermittently along the road were small roadside stands selling fresh fruit and vegetables, as well as the catch of the day. As they passed Fort Charlotte, which sat on a bluff overlooking the entrance to Nassau Harbour, Krueger said:

"Do you know that the United States occupied this island in 1776?"

"I did not know that," Wiegard replied.

"Oh, yes, " said Krueger. "George Washington sent troops to take over the island so the British could not use the harbour for supplies and ammunition. It was the first-ever American occupation of a foreign country. That was in 1776; this fort was built in 1789 after the American Revolutionary war. It was built to protect the island from that ever happening again."

Wiegard was impressed. This young man had clearly done his homework.

The car continued to wind its way west and Krueger took it all in as he rode in the back seat next to Wiegard.

Several minutes passed sitting in silence.

Krueger, looking around, turned to Wiegard. "Colonel Wilkinson speaks very highly of you, sir. He says you are a man of integrity and influence. He says that men like you can become targets for men of ill means and that the time is now to upgrade all of your security and intelligence."

"Well, I must remember to thank Colonel Wilkinson for those kind words.' Wiegard replied. "I don't know how much intelligence needs to be updated but my personal security certainly needs updating. I have several ventures in these islands, and of course, my personal residence. I travel all about, to and from your country. Certain projects require more attention than others. Your job will be to accompany me, assess the situation, make recommendations and implement them."

"You are the only member of your family that is in residence here, correct?" asked Krueger.

"That is correct. My wife and children are back home."

"Sounds easy enough," said Krueger. "I can take care of that."

The car turned into the driveway leading to Wiegard's personal residence.

CHAPTER TWELVE

Tuesday, September 9th, 1941
Blackwood Country Home
30 miles northwest of London

Thomas quickened his pace when he saw the car's headlight approaching from around a clump of trees. He had traveled from Colchester to the town of Wycombe, which was only an hour on the bus from London, where he had stopped off to make some inquiries.

His quiet little life had been disrupted ten days ago by the appearance of the strange Mr. Blackwood and his cloak and dagger routine.

The envelope Blackwood left him informed him that the bastards had never kicked him out of the army as they had promised. Something strange was going on and he was smack dab in the middle of it.

He tried to verify his orders while in London, but no one could help him. The official paperwork Blackwood had left him informed him that he was assigned to Special Group B and that he was to report to the address provided in the town of Wycombe. No one in London had ever heard of Special Group B.

The car slowed as it came closer. As it came to a stop next to Thomas, he realized that the driver was the same young man who had accompanied Blackwood back at the pub. The driver stared straight ahead. Thomas stood there momentarily and instinctively knew that the driver wasn't going to speak. Opening the door, he climbed into the back seat.

Gunning the engine several times, the driver made a half-turn and headed back in the direction from which he came.

Thomas examined the interior of the sedan and tried to catch the driver's eyes in the rear view mirror. He knew the young man posed no threat to him because he had the advantage of the superior position.

They drove on for about twenty minutes. As time passed, fewer and fewer homes appeared. What little light the few houses gave off was all there was and the night had a dense and dark sense to it.

The driver turned onto a private gravel drive that wound its way for a quarter of a mile up to a large, grey, two-story Tudor style house. It fit right into the natural landscape surrounding it. As the driver brought the car to a stop, the clash between the tired and gravel somehow seemed louder than normal to Thomas. His senses were on a high alert.

They had stopped in front of a single dark-brown door with two dim lights on either side.

Thomas wasn't surprised at how quickly the driver exited the vehicle and walked away in the other direction from the house. Exiting the vehicle himself, he looked around to get his bearings. The darkness of the night made seeing past ten feet impossible. Adjusting his eyes to the dark, he was about to knock when Oliver Blackwood opened the door. He was wearing a dark green cardigan and smoking a pipe.

"Welcome to my home, Mr. Nash. Please come in."

The old man stood aside and stretched his right arm out, inviting Thomas inside.

He smiled to himself. The pipe and cardigan combination made him look like a grandfather. Thomas wouldn't be lulled by appearances. "You're a strange old man and this is getting stranger as it continues," he said, walking inside.

Closing the door behind them, Blackwood said, "All will be explained, this way please." Behind a towering, solid wooden door, Blackwood led Thomas into a large, dark -- and long – room.

Thomas felt as if he'd stepped back outside into the darkness.

He could see the dark oak paneling and he could feel the frayed carpet under his feet. It was the only source of color.

"Please have a seat, Mr. Nash and we can get started," Blackwood said, gesturing toward an overstuffed chair. Taking their seats across from each other, Blackwood tapped the tips of his fingers together. Looking straight at him, Blackwood asked, "Would you care for something to drink?"

Thomas stared directly at Oliver Blackwood. Now it begins, he thought.

"I'm fine, thank you sir."

"Very well then," Blackwood said, still speaking over his pressed fingertips, "You had yourself quite a career going until you struck General Anderson. A most unfortunate incident, don't you think?"

"Is that was this is all about?" Thomas replied. "You are aware I served my time for that?"

"It is not about that incident per se; I'm just curious as to what type of man goes off and strikes a superior officer," Blackwood replied. "That's all."

"Is that what you want to know?' Thomas said, feeling the first hint of irritation. "Well I'll tell you what kind of a man goes off and strikes a superior officer. One who no longer feels that the officer in question is superior."

"I see." Blackwood paused. "And you determined this for yourself, single-handedly, that this officer was no longer superior, as you say?"

"I'm not going to play this little game with you," Thomas replied, running short on patience. "Position and rank have nothing to do with competency. This system of promotion through one's social class has given us weak military leaders and if you are half as intelligent as I think you are, you already know that."

"Regardless of one's intelligence or beliefs," answered Blackwood, "Striking a superior officer indicates a breakdown in authority and in the system of rank and order. That would lead to an even more chaotic environment, wouldn't you agree?"

"Look, Mr. Blackwood. I don't have any regrets. General Anderson is a fool and his leadership was downright treasonable. Now, I don't need to have a system of rank and order as you say to tell me if someone is doing a good job. General Anderson cost many men their limbs and their lives. I'd smack the bastard again if he were standing here right now."

Booming laughter erupted behind him. Thomas sprung to his feet, swinging himself around…he came face to face with Winston Churchill.

The Prime Minister was dressed in a three-piece, navy blue pinstripe suite. He held an unlit cigar in his left hand. Churchill had been there all along.

"Mr. Prime Minister, it is an honor to meet you," Thomas said, having recovered from his initial surprise.

"Honor is for the dead; it is my great pleasure to meet you," replied Churchill, accepting Thomas's out stretched hand. "Please take your seat and I hope you will join me for a drink."

Oliver Blackwood produced a bottle and three glasses, filling each glass halfway. Churchill spent a few moments lighting his cigar. It gave Thomas time to gather his thoughts. The situation had gone from the strange to the bizarre.

"I cannot say I wouldn't have smacked General Anderson myself," Churchill began. "He's not my type of general -- a bit pompous, nevertheless -- that is in the past and we are here to speak about the future."

Thomas sat back and listened.

The bloody Prime Minister of Great Britain was sitting across from him and wanted to discuss the future. *What was going on?*

Reaching for his drink, Churchill broke the silence. "I have taken more out of alcohol than alcohol has taken out of me. Drink up, Mr. Nash; we have much to discuss this evening."

Thomas smiled, albeit slightly. At least the Prime Minister seemed like an ordinary fellow: regardless of the outcome of this meeting, he was going to need a drink.

"I will drink with you, sir," he replied, toasting the Prime Minister. "To Britain."

"To Britain," Churchill said, refilling his glass. Oliver Blackwood sat back in his chair. His drink lay untouched.

"I suppose you are wondering what you are doing in the middle of the night and in the country home of an old friend of the Prime Minister's?" asked Churchill.

"Well, the thought had crossed my mind," replied Thomas, oddly comfortable with his sarcastic retort.

Churchill smiled, grunted, and puffed on his cigar.

"You know Mr. Nash, when I am abroad, I always make it a rule never to attack the government of my country. I make up for lost time when I come home."

Churchill turned and faced Thomas.

"There are those in our government who do not wish us success in our great struggle. Most of these people are insignificant, but some of these people are downright treacherous and dangerous. Some hold positions of power and great influence. I know that you understand what I mean. I know your bitter experiences. But I also know that you love your country and that if called to serve, you will with unquestioned loyalty."

"I never wanted to stop serving my country," Thomas replied, eyeing Churchill directly. "This General Anderson business just got in the way."

Churchill smiled. "Well, that's out of the way and your services are now needed." Churchill downed his second glass and continued turning to Blackwood. "I am never going to have anything more to do with politics or politicians when this war is over. I shall confine myself entirely to writing and painting." Turning back towards Nash, he asked, "Are you a religious man, Mr. Nash?"

"I don't think about it much. I've seen some bloody awful things that would make one question a divine existence, but these things are beyond me."

"There's an old Russian proverb that says, God gave man the truth, the Devil organized it and called it religion," Churchill said. "The better question, Mr. Nash, is are you a man of faith?"

Thomas thought about it. "Mr. Prime Minister, I have tremendous faith but in only a few things. I have faith in my ability; I have faith that my country for all its faults is still the right leader and example of and to the world. I have faith that somehow we will prevail in these struggles because I suppose that I have faith good will triumph over evil."

"Do you have faith in our institutions … in our, shall we say, British way of life?" asked Churchill, sitting forward in his chair.

"I do, sir. I believe we are an advanced society, destined to run the world and I believe our form of government and society while not perfect are by far superior."

Churchill raised an eyebrow, "Do you have faith in my judgment?"

Thomas was surprised by this question.

"I think you are the right man in the right place at the right time," he replied. "I don't envy your job but I do have confidence in your leadership."

"Leadership sometimes requires one to do things that can be personally distasteful." Churchill said, puffing on his cigar. "But I have learned to live with these decisions." Fixing his gaze on Thomas, he continued. "Let me not beat about the bush, Mr. Nash. I want to use your skills and experience on a most secretive and clandestine mission. I want to send you to determine if one of our own is truly a traitor and if what we have been made aware of is true. If it is true, I want you to terminate the subject."

The Prime Minister sat back in his chair and took a drink from his glass.

Thomas was dissatisfied. He was missing information. Surely, Mr. Churchill and his Mr. Blackwood could find able men in the armed services more than capable of doing this kind of work.

"What has this alleged traitor done to warrant such a absolute solution?" he asked, meeting the Prime Minister's gaze.

Churchill cleared his throat and growled. "He has violated every oath he has ever taken. He is responsible for leaking military plans to the Germans. He has conspired to assist our enemies with advice on how to defeat us and he has set into motion a plan to kidnap, as well as either kill or ransom, the Royal Princesses." Pausing to allow his words to resonate, he continued.

"Any one of these acts is reason enough but to strike at one's own nieces in an attempt to hurt one's brother and to help the Nazis by further demoralizing this nation is completely over the line and unacceptable."

Thomas knew immediately that the Prime Minister was referring to Edward the Duke of Windsor. "Are you telling me that the Duke of Windsor wants to kidnap the royal Princesses?"

"That is exactly what I am telling you. And who knows what his plans are for them after he's got them."

"And you want me to do exactly what ... determine if any of this is true and then, if it is true ... what ... kill the Duke?" asked Thomas.

"With malice!" Churchill replied.

Thomas hesitated momentarily and then burst into a fit of laughter surrounded by silence.

"The whole thing sounds like it's out of a mystery novel," he said, after he had stopped laughing. "The only problem is that I know you're quite serious and yet I can't help but laugh at how absurd it all sounds. Why not just arrest the bastard and charge him with crimes?"

Churchill leaned forward in his chair, "This is not official, this is not authorized, how could it be? No, Mr. Nash, this is a decision I have made and I have chosen you to complete this mission. The three of us in this room are the only ones who know of what we speak."

Thomas sat back and exhaled. "So it's all unauthorized?"

"Absolutely off the record." Churchill replied.

"Why me? Why do I deserve this honor?"

Churchill puffed on his cigar. "Mr. Nash, deep down inside you are a decent and good man and you understand the ways of the world. You not only have the ability and the training to conduct this mission but you also have the right makeup." The Prime Minister shifted in his chair and continued. "You struck General Anderson even though you knew it would cost you. It was the right thing to do, the honorable thing to do -- that is the main qualification. This country is in a fight for its ultimate survival and I am sworn to defend it to the death. The Duke poses a great threat to our survival and I want that threat eliminated. Will you help me?"

Thomas already knew the answer to that question, he was being asked to serve and he would serve. But he didn't know if he could actually kill the Duke. Killing in battle is one thing, but this? This was personal. My God, he thought, he was going to kill a king.

"Of course I will help you, Prime Minister. Now, where do we begin?"

Churchill's face broke out into a big smile, and he huffed his approval. "Good! Now let's have another drink."

Thomas stole a quick glance at Oliver Blackwood. Blackwood, not smiling, stared directly at him. Nash couldn't help but feel that Blackwood knew what he was thinking.

CHAPTER THIRTEEN

Friday, September 26th, 1941
Hog Island

It had taken Wiegard nearly a month to bring Krueger to Hog Island. As he piloted the launch towards the dock partially hidden by mangrove trees, he admitted to himself that he admired the young man's discipline. Krueger had asserted himself over all of Wiegard's Nassau assets.

Still, Wiegard remained unsure. The young American had only dealt with the household staff and the small clerical staff he kept in his downtown office on Elizabeth Avenue. Teaching the maids and the secretaries how to fend off an attacker and James how to drive faster didn't give him any indication as to how Krueger would respond under pressure.

Wiegard no longer had the luxury of time. He had been summoned to Germany by Grand Admiral Raeder to consult on the construction of the hydraulic catapult system he had designed. The catapult system was the major hardware component of the weapon system developing on Hog Island.

Wiegard couldn't quite ignore the voice in his head that told him his future was tied to his design.

He was preparing to leave for New York in two days, to make his way to Germany for the meeting. He had explained to Krueger that this was a personal trip and that he would have to stay in Nassau. This trip, Wiegard had explained, required Krueger to take over the security of Hog Island.

It was just past midnight, Wiegard's preferred time to visit the island. The scientists, of whom there were six, worked in shifts of two for eight hours at a time. Wiegard actually felt sorry for them. They were confined to the laboratory for ten hours a day and then they were only allowed out of the cave complex for one hour after dark. They worked like hamsters on a wheel and never once were there a complaint or request for any deviance.

All of their basic needs were supplied for months ago. They weren't interested in any festivities or distractions. Good Nazis, he thought to himself. Too bad they would all be dead when their work was done.

Krueger had finished tying up the motor launch after Wiegard navigated them to the hidden alcove and joined him on the shore.

"This island looks just like every other little atoll or rock in these waters, but this island holds a great treasure and I want you to guard it with your life," Wiegard said.

Kruger looked around and replied, "Unless there's gold buried here from some long lost pirate, I don't see much here to protect."

Wiegard laughed and lit a cigarette. He pointed to a line of pine trees that stood about twenty feet up from the water's edge.

"Past those trees, you will see." He paused and faced Krueger directly. "I have watched you this last month and I have been impressed. You are cut, as they say, from a superior piece of cloth, and so I am going to let you in on a little secret."

Krueger turned toward Wiegard and gave him his full attention.

"Germany is going to win this war." Wiegard began. "She is a superior country with superior people and a superior leader." Pulling on his cigarette, he continued. "Hitler represents the new Europe whilst Churchill and De Gaulle represent old Europe. The question is, you, you Americans. Where do you stand?"

Krueger shuffled his feet before answering. "Well I think the President has made it pretty clear that the United States is going to try to stay neutral."

"Ah, but neutrality may not be an option for long." Wiegard said. "And if one has to pick sides…"

"I would think that America, being a young country, would come down on the side of progressive ideas. Let's see what emerges from this conflict," Krueger replied.

"But you elected a feeble cripple to lead your country," Wiegard snapped. He could sense Krueger's reluctance to engage in this conversation. "Your Roosevelt is a man who makes Churchill look young. How can you compare your leader to the youth and vigor of Adolph Hitler?"

"American leaders come and go," Krueger replied, leveling his eyes to meet Wiegard's. "I think America is still a young country, compared to the European powers and I think my country could relate to the new ideas coming out of Germany, After all, we all share a common enemy in communism."

This answer had a calming effect on Wiegard. "Quite right, the Russians are the real scourges of the world. Right, follow me," he said, abruptly tossing his cigarette and walking toward the trees.

Wiegard led the way as they climbed up toward the tree line, the ground leveling out. He ducked into the trees and Krueger followed, immediately becoming aware of how dense and thick the bushy woods were. Pine trees provided a tremendous cover.

They continued walking through the trees as the land began to slope downward. Wiegard stopped as they reached a small clearing.

Two whitewashed buildings, almost indistinguishable from the sand, stood up against a large rock formation. "Do you see that large stone to the left of the buildings?" he asked Krueger, pointing to a spot across the clearing.

"I can make out those big boulders, if that's what you mean."

"Well, those rocks mark the entrance to a system of caves. Caves that house my most secret and dangerous work."

"This is your most secret and dangerous place and I don't see a single guard," Krueger remarked. "What is this?"

"I have only scientists who work here and I have two men who guard the entrance. I am bringing you in to take over because I must make this trip home and I need you to ensure that things go undisturbed here."

Wiegard had decided to let Krueger in without letting him know the true nature of the beast.

"You see, Mr. Krueger, chemicals can be very temperamental, like women, the right combination and things stay in control; the wrong combination and ...well ...boom."

"You're telling me that the scientists are working with chemicals that can blow up?" asked Krueger.

"That's why the lab is built into the caves," Wiegard said. "We don't need any accidents spreading." He immediately regretted using the word spreading and studied Krueger's face for any reaction.

"How long has it been operational?" Krueger asked.

"For some months now," Wiegard replied, watching Krueger go through his process. Wiegard had quickly learned how the young man operated. Krueger had been surveying the entrance to the cave complex and had been lining up site lines from the moment they stopped in the clearing.

"I want to spend some time sizing this situation up." Krueger said, turning toward Wiegard. "There are a lot of ways to come at this place; all right, I'll get on it. In the meantime, let's take a look in this cave."

Krueger led the way across the clearing. Wiegard followed him inside.

＝╬╪＝

Franklyn and Michael Gibson, two local 16-year-old boys, were rowing their way toward the western end of Hog Island on an adventure.

They were born exactly three months apart. Franklyn was the oldest, a fact he always teased Michael about. The boys also shared a family trait; both had deep blue colored eyes.

Michael's family had lived on Hog Island for as far back as Franklyn could remember. They were one of the main families to be relocated to Nassau after the government shut everything down. Franklyn, whose mother had died giving birth to him, lived with his father in

Nassau. He spent his summers on Hog Island with his cousin. The two were inseparable.

They had decided to sneak out of the house and sail over to Hog Island and 'have an adventure', as Franklyn put it. What was going on over at Hog Island? They were curious, and to them, it was a great mystery.

The boys used the natural current to propel them as they approached the western end of Hog Island – the island's narrowest point, a mere two miles from Nassau Harbor.

They secured the dinghy by dragging it half way up the beach and tying it to a coconut tree. It was low tide, so Franklyn adjusted the rope. The boys worked by the moonlight stowing the oars in the bottom of the boat and covering the Dinghy with some palm leaves. It was a poor job of camouflage, but after all, this was just an adventure.

After securing the boat the boys moved up the beach to the tree line and sat down underneath a row of 20-foot pine trees. From here, they could see the lights of Nassau Harbor.

"Feel good to be home, eh?" Franklyn asked.

Michael didn't answer and Franklyn didn't expect one; Michael didn't speak much.

"Man I can't believe they done moved you all out like that; we had so much fun in this place. Remember when we used to hide out in them caves and your daddy caught us with his bottle o' rum?" Franklyn asked.

"We used to do all kind tings in them caves. I wonder what they doin' with them caves today?" replied Michael.

"Some strange things goin' on." Franklyn continued. "All these empty islands around here and they gotta move people out of this one ... it don't make no sense."

They spent a few more minutes dazing around and then Franklyn got up.

"Let's go boy," He said, leading the way into the bush and to a well-worn path that trans versed the entire island. Franklyn had calculated it would take less than an hour to hike to the entrance to the caves, located in the middle of the island.

The boys spoke very little for the first fifteen minutes of the hike. Each was in tune with his own thoughts as Hog Island had deep meaning for both of them. They were also used to going long periods without speaking. After all, fishing required silence and the boys had spent most of their lives fishing together.

After a half hour passed, Franklyn stopped. The incline had slowly been increasing. He didn't realize it, but from this point forward, their hike would be over the cave complex.

"We gon be at the cave mouth in about ten minutes," said Franklyn. "We need to come up on it easy like...we don't know what goin' on over here so we need to be careful."

"I know," replied Michael. "When the ground start risin' up toward that line of Pine trees dat opposite the cave, let me go in front...I know that path better than you I isn't gon slip up or make any noise."

"All right," replied Franklyn after a moment of hesitation. He had always been the leader of their little adventures and Michael had never asserted himself before. "Let's keep goin'." He said.

The boys continued single-file along the path, changing positions along the way. As they approached the center of the island, trees started to thin out. Michael led the way toward a clump of bush and trees that had a good view of the cave entrance and provided some cover.

Taking up positions at the base of a half dozen pine trees rooted together on a small ridge, Franklyn pulled out an old leather lined canteen and he and Michael each drank from it before settling in to their viewing positions.

Michael shinnied up one of the pine trees and climbed out onto one of the branches. This afforded him a better view of the cave entrance but also allowed him to see around the large rock formation, which would help him spot anyone approaching from that way.

For the first ten minutes the boys saw nothing. Franklyn was just beginning to relax a bit when the first guard appeared. The solitary sentry was dressed in a dark green jump suit and had a rifle slung over his shoulder. He moved slowly across the front of the cave entrance and took up a position on the far right of the clearing. The second guard appeared a couple of minutes later. As he came out of the cave entrance, two white men exited behind him.

The first guard joined the group. Franklyn could hear their mumbled voices but none of their conversation could be understood. The four men continued conversing and Franklyn and Michael remained frozen in their hiding places.

As if struck by lightning and with a loud "crack," the tree branch that Michael was laying on came crashing down. Michael tumbled from twenty feet above and struck the ground with a thunderous force. The silence was broken.

Horrified and shocked, Franklyn watched the two white men and guards spring into action.

Scrambling over to his cousin, he found him moaning as he lay in a crumpled lump clutching at his right ankle. His head had missed a large rock by mere inches. Grabbing him around the shoulders, he hoisted Michael to a sitting position.

"Get up Michael, we got to go," Franklyn said, struggling to help his cousin to his feet.

"I can't walk, I broke up my foot," Michael responded, his breathing coming in short sweaty gasps.

"I'm gonna help you," said Franklyn. He wrapped Michael's arm around his shoulder and placed his right arm under Michael's left arm. They tried to move forward but Michael was dead weight, fighting to stay conscious.

They only made it a couple of steps when Michael let go and sank to the ground. Franklyn dropped to the ground as well and got up close to his cousin's face. He could hear the men climbing the ridge and knew that they would be upon them in a few minutes. Michael was slipping in and out of consciousness and he looked up and spoke to Franklyn.

"Run ... run, boy. Don't worry about me ... I'm a stay here and rest."

"No, man ... you gotta go with me," replied Franklyn.

"Look, I can't walk. Just cover me up and hide me and come back for me when the coast is clear."

"How the hell I ga hide you?" asked Franklyn, even more aware of the approaching men.

"Help me into that gully," said Michael, indicating a two-foot deep trench between two narrow rock formations. "You could cover me with some bush."

Franklyn knew that he had only a couple of minutes at best. Michael was right; this was the best plan. He moved quickly and with Michael's feeble help he got him into the trench and proceeded to cover him with fallen palm tree branches.

"Alright, sit tight and I'll come back and get you when it's safe," said Franklyn. He patted his cousin on the head for good luck and then took off into the bush.

━◈┼ ┼◈━

"What the hell was that?" Wiegard yelled out.

"Either someone else is on this island or we still have a couple of hogs running loose," replied Krueger, drawing a pistol from his belt. Barking at the guards, he ordered one of them to go left and the other to go right.

"I'll go up the middle," he finished yelling. "Give me a damn flashlight."

One of the guards handed Krueger his flashlight and the three men began to slowly climb up to the ridge from where the noise had come from.

Wiegard followed Krueger and the two guards up to the top of the ridge and the four men spread out looking in all directions. The woods were quiet except for the natural noises of crickets and other insects.

Krueger turned and looked back down toward the cave entrance. "You see now why you have to have a guard up here? You always take the high ground, how come you didn't know that?" Krueger said, addressing one of the shrugging guards. "Alright, let's fan out and search the area."

Wiegard followed Krueger closely behind. He didn't have a gun on him and he cursed himself under his breath. Krueger had produced one instantly. He made a mental note to never be caught again without a gun.

One of the guards made his way over to the area where a fresh tree branch had fallen.

Wiegard watched as the guard was using the end of his rifle to poke and prod at the bushes and fallen debris on the ground. The guard turned and headed directly to the edge of a Gully and started prodding the ground with his rifle barrel.

Wiegard had looked away and did not see the guard discover the boy, but he responded to the guard's yelling and turned, to see the guard holding his rifle to the head of a young black boy laid out on the ground.

Wiegard and Kruger moved to where the guard stood with his rifle pointed straight at his captive. Wiegard could see that the boy was terrified, panting heavily and unable to move.

The guard lowered his weapon. "Get him up," Krueger ordered.

The guard yanked the young boy up to a kneeling position.

Krueger looked down at the boy and addressed him. "What is your name?"

The boy did not reply.

"What are you doing here?"

Again, the boy didn't respond. Wiegard could see the terror in the boy's eyes.

Slapping the boy across the face, with the back of his hand, Krueger asked him again, "I said, what are you doing here?"

"I, I, used to live here." The boy stammered.

"Are you alone?"

"Yeah, I come by myself."

"I see," said Krueger. "Let him go," he said to the guards, who loosened their hold on the boy, allowing him to slump down into the ground.

Without warning, Krueger drew his pistol, pointed it at the boy's head and pulled the trigger. The shot stunned Wiegard and the two guards. It was sudden and brutal.

Krueger turned and locked eyes with the shocked Wiegard, "Take the body into the cave," he ordered the guards.

Wiegard noted the calmness in Krueger's stare.

The two guards hesitated, still in shock, finally picking up the boy's lifeless body and starting their way down the ridge toward the caves.

Krueger remained calm and composed. This young American had it after all, Wiegard thought to himself. Krueger was ruthless enough for the job. He could leave for Germany and his secret meeting with Admiral Raeder. Assured Hog Island would be in good hands; Wiegard lit a cigarette as he made his way down the ridge and back to the cave entrance.

CHAPTER FIFTEEN

June 5th, 2013
Katherine Blackwood's Sitting Room

Nicholas sat in silence absorbing everything that Katherine had told him. Franklyn was the same man whose cousin Michael had been murdered on Hog Island. The brutality of it shocked him.

"Tell me about this Krueger character," Nicholas asked after a few more minutes of silence.

"What do you want to know?" replied Katherine.

Nicholas could tell she was getting tired but he knew the evening had just begun.

"Well he was obviously a cold hearted killer and he had a German Sir name, was he a Nazi sympathizer like Wiegard, was he a German?"

"No," Katherine said. "He was an American of German heritage and he was forced to kill Michael."

"What do you mean forced? He could have let the boy live."

"He could have," Katherine replied. "But that would not have been in keeping with his role."

"His role. What role he was playing?"

"A very important one," Katherine said. "In fact, Krueger was the one who found the proof that really set this whole saga on its heels."

"I am not sure I am following you."

Katherine, as if reading his mind said, "I know this is all a bit confusing but you will see in the end that Krueger was a good man."

"A good man!" Nicholas said, his voice rising in anger. "He shot and killed a 16-year-old boy. How can you call him a good man? I'll bet Franklyn does not think him a good man."

Katherine's face was stoic in response.

"Franklyn has been a front row witness to the cruelty of fate and of man. He knows the truth and he still weeps for his cousin Michael, but he understands; after all of these years, he understands." Katherine paused for a moment. "Krueger, well, he was a good man because like other good men he did what he had to do."

"This seems to be a constant theme of yours," Nicholas said, letting his exasperation come through.

"All of these so called good men, doing such terrible things."

"Now you are beginning to understand. That is precisely the lesson I am trying to teach you. Just because someone does something reprehensible does not make him or her a bad person, especially if that horrible action was in the service of the greater good. Killing Michael was a tragedy, but it had to be done."

"Had to be done?" Nicholas said, almost spitting the words out, "I don't think killing an innocent 16-year-old boy ever has to be done no matter what strange code of behavior you subscribe to," rubbing his temple with his thumb and forefinger he continued, "I mean a 16-year-old boy shot in the head at point-blank range, what the hell is wrong with you? Can't you see how very wrong that is?"

Katherine waited a few minutes before responding, "I know how cold and calculating it sounds and believe me when I tell you that none of this is acceptable until you weigh the alternative and what would have come to pass if not for these unthinkable acts." She paused allowing Nicholas a moment with his thoughts and then continued, "Time has not changed my dismay at these horrors, in fact I alone have borne this knowledge and it has not been easy but I assure you that in the end, there was no alternative."

"Franklyn, your Franklyn; he is the same Franklyn, right?" asked Nicholas.

"The same."

"How did he get here?"

"Franklyn is the one saving grace from this whole episode. I believe his survival was the one act that saved my grandfather and allowed him to keep his humanity."

Nicholas murmured to himself, "I don't understand."

"You will, my boy. You will," Katherine replied, her voice drifting off.

CHAPTER SIXTEEN

Tuesday, September 30th, 1941
Nassau, Bahamas

It had been three days since Franklyn escaped from Hog Island. Michael had never appeared. When Franklyn finally let the story out to his father and aunt Edith, his father James lashed out. Franklyn took refuge behind his aunt.

"I can't believe you damn fools went over to Hog Island," Franklyn's father roared. "You know damn well ain't nobody suppose to be over there. Where the hell you think your cousin gone to?"

"I don't know, Daddy," he said, still hiding behind his aunt who was rocking back and forth by this time chanting under her breath. "But while I was running away, I heard a gunshot!"

With these words, Michael's mother broke into a loud wail.

The screams and commotion continued for a few minutes until finally Franklyn's father raised his voice and ordered silence. The group settled down and only a low murmur of whimpering cries could be heard.

"I ga go see Commissioner Atkinson," James said. "The rest of y'all need to fan out and look for Michael but don't anybody go near Hog Island. Franklyn, come with me boy."

With those words, he started walking toward town and the police commissioner's office. Franklyn fell in five steps behind his father still wary of his anger.

Police Commissioner Atkinson's office was on East Street just off the main road and across the square from the courts. The building was a single-story concrete structure, bright yellow and with huge windows that opened to the street and allowed the air to circulate. Locals were known to hang out in the waiting room of the police station during particularly hot days because the coolness of the concrete and the cross breeze.

Franklyn and his father walked in the front door and were greeted by a constable asleep in his chair behind the long counter that ran the width of the room. Franklyn's father slammed his hand down on the counter, startling the young policeman.

"Wake up, man," James said, showing his irritation with the sleeping constable. "Where Commissioner Atkinson is? I need to speak with him."

"He should be coming back any moment now," replied the young constable. "He just run over to court for something or the other, he ain't ga be long."

"Well I ain't leaving 'till I talk to the man. So we ga sit right here till he come back." Franklyn took a seat on a bench on the opposite side of the room.

Fifteen minutes passed and Commissioner Atkinson walked into the station, papers in hand.

The young policeman was on his feet immediately and looked at Franklyn's father before announcing to the commissioner that he had visitors. James and Franklyn had gotten up from their seats as soon as the commissioner walked in the door but as was the custom, they waited for the commissioner to address them.

Atkinson turned around and immediately recognized James and Franklyn as members of the families that had been displaced from Hog Island.

"What can I do for you?"

"Well, sir," James began. "My nephew has gone missing and his mother is all crazy like."

"Missing?" replied the Commissioner. "How can anyone go missing on this island? It's too damn small."

"Well, sir," James stammered, intimidated by the commissioner's presence. "He and Franklyn here was over to Hog Island and…"

"Hog Island!" exclaimed the Commissioner. "You know damn well that no one is supposed to be on Hog Island. What the devil was ya doing there, lad?"

"We thought it would be fun to row over there and just look around the old place." Franklyn stammered. "We was just funning and then something happened."

"Well, what happened?" the Commissioner asked.

"We came up on the ridge, you know the part that does lead up above the caves and, they was these men mulling around the caves and they had… guns and tings."

"Go on," Atkinson said, his interest aroused. Wiegard and the Duke's explanations as to why Hog Island needed to be evacuated had never satisfied him.

"Ya see," continued Franklyn. "Michael …he did climb up a tree and just when all them men was outside the cave, the branch broke and Michael fell down and broke up his foot. Those men heard all that racket and they start running and climbing up the ridge to where we was. Michael was hurt bad and he couldn't put any stress on his foot and he told me to go and that he was ga hide." Franklyn's words were coming more rapidly now as he poured out the story to the Commissioner. "I did run as fast as I could and after about fifteen minutes I climbed up a tree to hide and see if I could figure out what to do…. and that's when…" Franklyn paused.

"When what?" asked the Commissioner

"When I heard the gun shot."

The Commissioner took all of this in and then after a moment asked, "Are you sure it was a gun shot?"

"Yes sir," Franklyn said, struggling to hold back the tears. "I knows that sound from when I go hunting with my Daddy."

"Well then what happened?"

"I waited about an hour up that tree and then just before the sun was coming up I made my way back to the western tip where we had left the boat and I rowed back to Nassau."

"When did all of this occur?" asked the Commissioner.

"Night before last," answered Franklyn.

"And your cousin has not returned home?"

"No, ain't nobody seen him," James responded. "My family is out looking for him but I already told them not to go to Hog Island."

"Alright," said the Commissioner, turning his attention back to Franklyn and his father. "I'll look into it. In the meantime, stay away from Hog Island."

Franklyn's father nodded his acceptance to the Commissioner and grabbed Franklyn by the hand and led him out of the door.

CHAPTER SEVENTEEN

Friday, October 10th, 1941
Nordseewerke Naval Shipyard
Emden, Germany

R olf Wiegard was on German soil. He had arrived at the Nordseewerke Shipyard in Emden the previous night after crossing the Atlantic aboard a cargo ship that steamed out of New York five nights earlier. The ship had docked in Southampton England and had been met by agents of the German spy network who operated in England. Immediately, they whisked him to another smaller vessel that departed port as soon as Wiegard was on board. This small craft, navigating at night, had deposited him at the Nordseewerke shipyard.

He had spent the night in a small apartment above one of the large warehouses that housed parts and materials. Wiegard noted that the place was perfect for a person conducting an illicit affair since it was so difficult to detect in the larger scale of the building.

He had not slept well, a combination of his six -day journeys, and his anticipation and trepidation of this morning's meeting. He has spent the last hour writing his thoughts down in his leather journal.

The meeting with Grand Admiral Raeder was scheduled for 7:30. Freshly shaved and wearing a dark gray suit, Wiegard sat on the bed. He had been awake for several hours already.

Three rapid knocks on the door broke the silence.

"Herr Wiegard, are you awake?" The voice belonged to the German soldier who had escorted him to the small apartment the previous night.

"Yes, I am ready," Wiegard replied, rising and opening the door.

The guard had accompanied him alone last night but this morning there were four guards and Wiegard immediately suspected that something was different.

"I see you have some company this morning," Wiegard addressed the guard.

"You are an important person Herr Wiegard. Do you not warrant such an escort?" the guard replied, his lips breaking into a sly smirk.

Wiegard paused briefly and tried to decipher his meaning.

"Very well. I am ready to proceed, shall we?" he said, walking past the original guard and onto the top landing of the stairs that led up to the small apartment.

The two guards in the front turned and began walking down the stairs. Wiegard fell in behind them and the original guard along with the fourth member of the group brought up the rear. He was surrounded, and as the group proceeded down the stairs and onto the floor of the large warehouse, it occurred to Wiegard that his little party looked more like a prison transport than an escort.

At the bottom of the stairs the original guard moved to the front of the pack and without anyone speaking, they crossed the entire length of the warehouse. As they approached the large double doors that Wiegard had entered through the previous night, the guard turned to his left and entered a stairwell. These stairs descended in a straight line into a subterranean basement area. As the group of guards all got closer together due to the limitation of the stairwell, Wiegard broke out into a cold sweat.

His mind was racing. *Was this the end? Where did I go wrong or is my success my undoing?* All of these things were rolling around in his brain when the party reached the bottom of the stairs and entered a large room with two large heavy steel doors on the opposite side.

Before Wiegard could adjust his vision, he felt the presence of more soldiers. A voice called out:

"Achtung, state your purpose."

Snapping to attention, the original guard spoke.

"Sergeant Schmidt, delivering Herr Wiegard for a meeting."

Wiegard was struck by the guard's name as he thought it might be one of the last names he would ever hear. A slight bead of perspiration had formed on his forehead but he refused to wipe his brow.

Sergeant Schmidt stepped aside and Wiegard came face-to-face with the owner of the voice he had heard commanding the attention of the sergeant.

A tall, thin blonde-haired German officer dressed in the black SS uniform stared at Wiegard with the deepest green eyes he had ever seen.

"You are Herr Rolf Wiegard, correct?" asked the SS officer, seemingly reading his name from a black leather journal.

"I am," replied Wiegard.

"I knew your father," said the officer, snapping the journal shut and handing it off to a subordinate.

Wiegard was very surprised at this statement and stammered a response.

"My father died over 25 years ago, you must have been very young, Herr Captain."

"I was a mere boy. My father was an engineer like your father and once, when I was 8, we took a holiday in your country and my father took me with him when he visited your father's workshop."

The mention of his father's workshop took Wiegard back in time. He smiled.

"You are embarrassing me, Herr Captain. I have very fond memories of my father's workshop. I used to play outside with my friends and we always had to be very quiet so as not to disturb my father's work."

"I remember," said the German captain. "I sat on your father's work bench looking out of the window at some boys playing in the street while my father and your father talked. I wonder if you were one of those little urchins I saw playing?"

"Quite possibly."

"Very well. Search him," commanded the Captain, his tone quickly slipping back into efficiency.

Two new guards from the SS captain's detail quickly grabbed a hold of Wiegard and expertly ran their hands over every inch of him. When they were finished, they stood back and Wiegard once again was face-to-face with the SS Captain.

The captain turned toward the large metal doors behind him. He knocked three times on the door and it opened ever so slightly. The Captain leaned into whatever was beyond the door. Wiegard could hear muffled conversation but could not understand anything.

After a couple of minutes, the SS Captain turned back around and motioned for Wiegard to enter past him into the room. The Guard gestured with his arm for Wiegard to pass through. Wiegard hesitated and then walked into a large warehouse-sized room.

There were several people standing around and as the door closed behind him and his eyes adjusted to the dim lighting, Rolph Wiegard realized that the figure standing at the center of the conference table was Adolph Hitler.

His throat went completely dry and he struggled to swallow. Grand Admiral Raeder approached him.

"Good morning Herr Wiegard. You look like you have seen a ghost."

"I ... I, I did not expect to see the Fuhrer here."

"Of course not," Raeder responded. "Prudence does not allow us to reveal the Fuhrer's schedule but he has asked to see you personally. This is your moment, Herr Wiegard. Are you ready to meet the Fuhrer?"

Wiegard opened his mouth but no words came out. He nodded.

"Very well," said Raeder, turning back toward the conference table. "Come along."

Wiegard followed the Grand Admiral and they approached the conference table.

Hitler was standing at the center of the table: spread out in front of him was the blueprints of Wiegard's hydraulic launch system. The Fuhrer was inspecting the plans and Grand Admiral Raeder waited for the appropriate moment to address his leader.

Wiegard was happy for the delay and he forced himself to swallow. He did not want to stumble now, not at this moment. Hitler looked up from the plans and his gaze met Raeder's.

"My Fuhrer," began Raeder. "May I introduce Herr Rolf Wiegard?"

Raeder stepped aside and Wiegard was face to face with Hitler. His right arm instinctively extended into the Nazi salute and he rasped,

"Heil Hitler."

A wry smile creased Hitler's lips. "I have been reviewing your drawings, Herr Wiegard and I am struck by their simplicity," Hitler said, waiving Wiegard's salute down with a flick of his wrist.

Wiegard did not know how to respond. Was he being complimented, or criticized?

"I hope that they meet your approval, Mein Fuhrer," he finally uttered.

"They do, Herr Wiegard. I wish my officers thought as clearly and directly as your plans indicate. I am specifically impressed with how you disguise this, what do you call it ... a Catapult system. It is disguised right out in the open," Hitler said, pointing to a spot on the blueprints.

Wiegard had designed and perfected a launching mechanism that could be mounted on the side of a U-Boat. The mechanism used his latest developments in both hydraulics and vacuum technology.

This machine, aptly disguisable as part of the U-Boat's normal equipment, was capable of launching a projectile from the water with an accurate range of one mile. It was true that the U-Boat would have to surface to conduct the launch, but only for a short period of time. The skill and experience of the U-Boat captain would have to come into play.

"I thought it would help in camouflaging the launch mechanism if I could make it look like part of the rail system of the boat itself," Wiegard said.

"Very clever, very clever indeed," Hitler replied. "And the weapon, the weapon itself, where is that housed?'" asked the Fuhrer, turning the blueprints toward Wiegard.

Wiegard relaxed ever so slightly. He was confident in his work and his design.

"The missile is encased in a rubber bladder and attached to the base of the U-boat's conning tower. By strapping at least two missiles, camouflaged like that, you create symmetry and thus a natural look to the vessel. No one will look twice."

Hitler continued to study the blueprints in silence. The blood in Wiegard's head now started pounding and although the room was silent, he felt as if a train was bearing down in his head.

Hitler raised his gaze and stared directly into Wiegard's eyes. He held the look for a very long moment and then spoke.

"Tell me, Herr Wiegard ... Did any of my naval officers ask you to house the weapon on the outside of the hull?"

"I don't understand the question, Mein Fuhrer?" The pounding had now materialized in beads of sweat oh his forehead.

"My officers," said Hitler, indicating Admiral Raeder with a wave of his hand. "Did any of them ask you to design this system so that the missile would not be inside the U-boat?"

"No, no Mein Fuhrer. No officers interfered. It was simpler to load the missile into the catapult mechanism -- quicker and more efficiently from the deck. I thought it would take too much time to bring the weapon up from below and the boat would be exposed for too long."

Hitler continued to lock his gaze into Wiegard's eyes and Wiegard could tell that the German leader was trying to determine in his own mind if this Swiss engineer was telling the truth. Admiral Raeder stood to the side of the conference table and he had not moved a single inch during the entire exchange between Wiegard and the Fuhrer.

Without breaking his gaze, Hitler continued. "I am sometimes surrounded by lesser men, Herr Wiegard, men who do not think boldly and clearly as you do, men who do not have the stomach for the uniform they wear." Finally breaking his gaze, he continued. "My officers were the ones who insisted on Hog Island. They thought it would feed my ego to have an operation like that ongoing in a British crown colony, but I know the truth."

He looked in Admiral Rader's direction. "They are afraid to cross the Atlantic with chemical weapons on board so they maneuvered things to have the weapon developed by you in the Bahamas. That way, the chemical weapons would only be on board for a short amount of time."

Hitler folded the blueprints over on themselves before continuing. "I agreed to their plans because I want them to succeed and I have found eliminating as many reasons for failure as one can ensures the greater probability of success." Casting a glance in Admiral Raeder's direction and then back at Wiegard, he said, "So, I ask you again Herr Wiegard, did any of my officers ask that the weapon be stored on the exterior of the boat?"

Wiegard swallowed hard. "No, mein Furher, no officer asked for this. The decision was mine alone, based on making the launch process as efficient as possible."

Hitler locked eyes with Wiegard. The moment was an eternity and he could feel the perspiration on his neck freeze.

Relaxing his gaze, Hitler said. "I believe you Herr Wiegard. I have been so disappointed in my officers lately that I felt compelled to ask."

Wiegard stole a quick glance towards Admiral Raeder, when the Fuhrer turned his head. The German Admiral showed no reaction.

"So tell me, Herr Wiegard, how are the Duke and Mrs. Windsor getting along down there on that little island?" Hitler asked, walking around the large conference desk toward him.

"They are waiting, sir, for the inevitable outcome of this conflict."

"Walk with me, Herr Wiegard."

Wiegard sensed some movement by the officers behind him but he paid it very little attention and fell in step with the Fuhrer. They walked in silence for a few moments until they reached the far end of the warehouse. Hitler turned and faced back toward where Admiral Raeder and his staff were looking very busy and spoke.

"As soon as the Duke abdicated the throne, he regretted his mistake. At the outbreak of war, he was extremely helpful. He wants us to return him to power and I intend to accommodate his wishes."

"Their Majesties will be very pleased to hear that Mein Fuhrer," Wiegard said.

"I imagine so," Hitler said. "The thirst for power is unquenchable and the Duke walked away, something I could never understand. I will return him to his throne but he will serve me, not his people."

Hitler shuffled his feet and then spoke, almost to himself.

"The British will be the easy part; it's the Americans. The Americans, they are the only ones that can stop me now. Their sheer size and manufacturing capability makes them the only opponent who could come close to matching the great German people."

He turned and faced Wiegard directly.

"My generals and the Luftwaffe have hindered me but I am always two steps ahead of everyone. Do you think I am fool enough to fight a war on two fronts?" he said, snapping his jaw shut. "But no! No they failed to subdue Britain and the time for Russia had come and I will not be deterred. Britain will be defeated, not by planes and bombs over London, but by a shot fired on the other side of the world."

Wiegard noticed the Fuhrer's brow starting to furl and as his voice raised so did the intensity of his words.

Pounding his right fist into his left palm, Hitler continued. "The people, the American people, are very naïve. This will be their undoing. They are pathetic and they have no respect for our power. They actually believe that they can avoid getting involved in, as they call it, another European conflict but that damn Roosevelt knows better, he knows that America and only America is diverse enough and has the raw man power and resources to compete with Germany. Roosevelt and Stalin, Roosevelt and Stalin," he repeated. "This cannot come to pass the Jew lover and the Bolshevik united against Germany. Never! Never, would I allow this to happen."

Lowering his voice, Hitler looked directly at Wiegard, who stood mesmerized by the Furher's rant, and whispered, "Roosevelt cannot be allowed to succeed in bringing America into this war and that, Herr Wiegard, is why I must strike first. That is why you will go down in history as a great servant to the Fatherland. You Herr Wiegard will fire the shot that will cripple America."

The beads of sweat were breaking on his forehead, but Wiegard dared not wipe his brow. The most prominent man in the world was at this very moment anointing him with greatness. He wanted to remember it forever.

"Your creation," continued Hitler, "along with the greatness of German scientists will stop America in her tracks. In two months' time we will launch two chemical missiles from two U-boats into the heart of Washington and New York City using your catapult. You, Herr Wiegard, will kill all of their political leaders as well as most of their military command. Without America, Britain will capitulate and then I will be free to deliver justice to the communist scourge."

These words snapped Wiegard out of his trance and their weight settled in on him in an instant. His mouth opened and the words tumbled out before he remembered to whom he was speaking.

"But, thousands upon thousands of innocent people will die."

Hitler turned and looked directly at Wiegard and with a smile, said, "Greatness is the willingness to pay that price. A single death is a tragedy, Herr Wiegard, a million deaths is a statistic. America must not enter into this war. By attacking them savagely on three fronts, we will accomplish this."

"On three fronts?" asked Wiegard.

"Three fronts" replied Hitler. "Washington to kill their political leaders, New York to cripple their financial system and Hawaii to destroy their naval power."

"Hawaii?" asked Wiegard, his confusion showing.

"Germany is not without friends," replied Hitler, "The Japanese are our ally and they have their own reasons for wanting to destroy the American Naval fleet in the Pacific. I am just wise enough to use that to the advantage of Germany."

Wiegard dropped his head to avoid the Fuhrer's eyes and said, "As always Mein Fuhrer, you are the wisest one."

A smile crossed Hitler's face; "Remember this coming date Herr Wiegard for it is the day that will change the world. Remember December 7th, 1941."

CHAPTER EIGHTEEN

'My God, Hitler was mad," Nicholas said, in a whisper. "He fully intended to kill thousands, maybe millions of people in a preemptive chemical strike against the Americans, it's almost unfathomable."

"There is a fine line between genius and madman," Katherine replied. "If you think about it, it was a brilliant plan and had it succeeded, America would have been decimated. Even though there would have been a tremendous desire to retaliate, there would not have been any ability to do so. By the time America would have regrouped and mounted a challenge to Germany,

Britain would have fallen. Remember, in 1941, America was not the power she is today."

"But she would have retaliated," Nicholas said, almost pleadingly.

"Undoubtedly," Katherine replied, getting up from the sofa and walking toward the back of the room. "But it would have taken time and Britain would not have survived without America.

"Unbelievable," Nicholas muttered to himself.

"Would you like a drink?" asked Katherine, opening a bottle of Sherry and pouring a glass.

"I think I could use one."

"Did Churchill have any inkling of any of this?" Nicholas asked, accepting a glass of Sherry from Katherine.

"No one anticipated this type of attack on America, not even Churchill. He was under no illusions that Hitler would use a weapon of such horrific capability but no one anticipated or imagined that it existed or that it could be launched from the sea."

"And Wiegard stood ready to do this?" asked Nicholas. "What ever happened to him?"

"Wiegard was more than ready to pull the trigger, as they say. There were many people like Wiegard in the world at that time, sociopaths drunk on the idea of their superiority and righteousness and willing to commit their souls to Hitler and his perverted visions."

"Yes, but did he survive?"

"Not only did he survive," Katherine answered, "but he flourished after the war and died an old and extremely wealthy man."

"But how?" Asked Nicholas. "I'm baffled by that."

"Because the Americans wanted him to survive, but we will get to all that, now, let me continue the story." Katherine sat back down on the sofa and indicated to Nicholas to take his seat.

CHAPTER NINETEEN

Friday, October 31ˢᵗ, 1941
Nassau Bahamas

Thomas Nash stood on the forward deck of the cargo ship that had transported him from New York to The Bahamas. It had been almost six weeks since his meeting with Churchill at Blackwood's country home and he had not spent more than five minutes out of Blackwood's presence since that time. The old man was thorough, extremely so, in preparing him for this mission.

He had worked Thomas's body, but more importantly, he had worked his mind.

Blackwood knew instinctively that Thomas was struggling with the mission. Killing an anonymous person was one thing, killing a King, quite another. Thomas for his part was aware of his own misgivings about the mission, but he would put them out of his mind and focus on the information and direction being given by Blackwood.

All of the preparation and background information was stored in his brain. Thomas already knew the layout of the island, its history and its people. As the cargo ship entered the mouth of the harbour, he could see the Union Jack flying over Government House, which sat on a hill overlooking Nassau harbour. At the sight of the Governor General's home, Thomas Nash's thoughts turned to murder.

His mission, as unofficial and illegal as it was, was to dig around, find proof of Edward's treachery, and eliminate him.

It was the proof that concerned Thomas. Blackwood had continued to talk in circles but Churchill was clear – crystal clear. He wanted Edward gone, done with. There was no going back in the Prime Minister's mind.

The cargo ship had finished tying up and Thomas descended from the top deck, gathered his gear and disembarked onto the hot concrete pavement. It was 10:30 in the morning and the bustle of the port spread out in front of him.

As soon as his feet hit the ground, he was surrounded by three or four local boys pitching their services and grabbing at his bags in the hopes of earning a few pence. One of the boys was a bit bigger than the others. He pushed his way to the front.

"Welcome to Nassau, sir. My name is Franklyn and if you will allow me I can assist you with your bags and tings."

Thomas was impressed with the young man's direct approach and handed over one of the bags and said.

"Right...very well then. I am looking for Commissioner Atkinson's office."

"Follow me sir; it just up the street here." Franklyn said, picking up Thomas's second bag, and leading the way away from the dock.

Thomas followed a few steps, looking around at the busy waterfront. The young boy carrying his bags had the most amazing blue eyes. What an unusual combination, he thought, blue eyes on a black face. Thomas sensed he was going to see a few more unusual things on this little trip.

He spotted her almost immediately. She was holding a single flower in her right hand with her back turned and her head cocked to the side. She was standing in front of a flower vendor's stall dressed in a cream colored suite and matching hat that seemed to light her presence to the whole world.

Thomas stopped in his tracks and on cue; Wallis Windsor turned her head and, from across the busy market square, locked eyes with him.

He could feel his blood pumping and for that brief moment before she looked away, the undeniable stirring in his loins. Amazing, he thought. He felt an almost electric connection.

It was over in a moment, and Wallis blended into the marketplace in the opposite direction leaving Thomas to catch himself and to catch up to Franklyn.

Crossing Bay Street, Thomas thought about how his mission had gotten a little more complicated: he was to widow a woman who had just stirred something primal in him.

Franklyn led the way up East Street to a bright yellow building.

Once inside, Franklyn put the bags down. "I ga wait here sir, Commissioner Atkinson's office down in the back. Ain't no constable on duty so you could just walk in and say hello."

Thomas looked at Franklyn and then at his bags. He still held the one small case in his hand but wondered about the other two.

"Don't worry, boss. I ga keep an eye on the bags it just that the commissioner don't take too kindly to us pestering the tourists and all so I just ga stay out da way"

Satisfied with that explanation, he continued, "Well, I'll be a few minutes with the Commissioner and then you can show me to my hotel."

Franklyn nodded as Thomas walked down the hall toward the Commissioner's office.

Commissioner Atkinson had his head buried in a file when Thomas knocked on the half-open door. The Commissioner looked up, closed the file he had been reading and rose from behind his desk.

"May I help you?" asked the Commissioner.

"I was looking for Commissioner Atkinson," Thomas replied.

"I'm Atkinson."

"Ah, well Commissioner Atkinson, I'm Thomas Nash," he began, "sent by his majesties Government to increase the production of citrus foods in these islands, to aid in the great fight back home." Extending his hand, Thomas easily slipped into the cover story that Oliver Blackwood had devised for him.

His cover involved a veteran who had been wounded at Dunkirk and was now unfit for active service. A little truth to a cover makes it easier to execute, Blackwood had reminded him. Thomas was alleged to have been a farmer before the war and in this manner he was continuing to serve his country.

The commissioner came from around the back of his desk and accepted Thomas's hand.

"I was just reading your file, Mr. Nash. London sent over your information last week. My gratitude for your service in France sir and my respect for you wanting to continue to serve."

"That's very kind of you, sir," Thomas said, a little taken aback by the commissioner's complimentary words.

"Please, sit down," the commissioner said as he returned to his desk chair. "Tell me Mr. Nash, how bad are things back home? What's going on the ground ... with the people?"

"They're catching hell commissioner," Thomas answered, settling into his seat. "The Germans bomb almost every night somewhere, somehow. The RAF are valiant, but it's an uphill struggle."

"Yes, yes I see," said Commissioner Atkinson as he leaned forward in his chair. "It's just that we are a bit isolated here in the Islands. Although we are domicile to His Royal Highness, not much happens. We really aren't part of this war."

"Well, that's why I'm here. His Majesty's Government needs to increase the production of citrus and these islands have the best soil to grow pineapples."

Thomas could sense that the Commissioner wasn't buying it. Maybe he was over thinking it or maybe it was an old military dog's instinct, either way, the Commissioner was suspicious. They locked eyes for a brief moment before the Commissioner looked away and spoke.

"The farms on this island are situated on the southwestern side. I will arrange for you to have a car so you can make your initial inspections."

"That would be greatly appreciated."

"I've cleared a small workspace for you in the back of the building, it's not much, but it's the best I can do unless you would like me to set you up in one of the two holding cells," Atkinson said with a wry smile. "You can set your office up in there tomorrow. I'll have them move a desk and a couple of chairs in; you'll feel right at home."

Rising from their seats simultaneously, the two men shook hands and locked eyes once again. Thomas was not yet used to his role and the older man's wariness registered on his face.

As Thomas exited the building, Franklyn picked up the bags.

"Where to, boss?"

"The Royal Victoria Hotel," Thomas replied.

Franklyn led the way east on Shirley Street toward the hotel. They walked in silence. Thomas was lost in his thoughts as he contemplated his mission. This was flesh and blood; it was here and now, and the image of Wallis crept back into his mind.

As they reached the entrance to the Royal Victoria Hotel yard, a large black sedan flying two flags on each front fender screeched to a halt in front of Thomas. Franklyn jumped to the curve and as Thomas turned toward the side of the car, he came face to face with Edward, Duke of Windsor --Governor General of the Bahamas -- the man he was sent to kill.

"An Englishman, look my dear. An Englishman," Edward called out from the backseat of the car.

Looking past Edward, Thomas's eyes once again his found Wallis's. The moment was broken as Edward exited the vehicle. The Governor General stood squarely in front of Thomas his hands clasped behind his back.

"Your majesty," Thomas said, bowing his head a nod.

"An Englishman, we said to our wife, An Englishman," Edward began. "As soon as we spotted you we knew by the way you carried yourself. Welcome, welcome. What is your name?"

"Nash, sir. Thomas Nash."

"Well, Mr. Nash. Are you here on pleasure or service?"

"Service, your majesty," Thomas answered, the irony of his true mission ringing in his brain.

"Ah wonderful," Edward continued, "We must have you to Government house to tell all. Are you going to be with us for a while?"

"For as long as it takes, I imagine," Thomas replied.

"Very well then," Edward said, nodding toward the Royal Victoria Hotel. "We see you are staying at Grand mama's namesake hotel, really the best place in town. We shall send for you. Good day, Mr. Nash."

"Good day, your majesty." As Edward climbed into the back seat of the car, Thomas looked for Wallis, but the Duchess had turned her head away.

Thomas shook his head as the car sped off. He needed a drink. He hadn't been on the island an hour and already he had come face to face with his target, and been laid low by the man's wife. Alcohol was definitely needed.

Opening the gate, Franklyn and Thomas climbed four large stone steps onto a large stone patio. There were tables and chairs strategically located under palm trees for shade and shelter. Several whicker sofas and seats surrounded the patio, each overflowing with multicolored cushions. There were several locals setting furniture and sweeping up leaves in preparation for the guests.

Thomas and Franklyn walked across the patio and entered the hotel lobby. A middle-aged black woman greeted Thomas and in a matter of a few minutes registered him into a room with a small verandah overlooking a side street that was lined with beautiful blooming bougainvillea.

Thomas entered the room on the second floor and threw his briefcase on the bed. Franklyn placed the rest of his bags on the floor as Thomas opened the verandah door and stepped out onto the small balcony. The view was limited and the street below was busy. A shrill car horn sounded as a small truck pushed its way through the alley. Thomas left the door to the verandah open and re-entered the room. He retrieved his wallet from inside his jacket pocket and removed a one-pound note.

"Tell me, lad," Thomas said. "Is there a bottle of whiskey to be had on this Island?"

"Mr. Duncomb at the corner store always got a bottle of rum or two but I ain't know about no whiskey, but I could ask," replied Franklyn, eyeing the one-pound note in Thomas's hand.

"Right then," said Thomas, handing the money over to Franklyn. "Rum or Whiskey. Whatever they have and be quick about it."

Franklyn took the note and scurried out the door.

"I'll be right back, boss," he said.

Thomas began unpacking his two larger cases -- some clothes in the closet and his toilet kit in the small bathroom. After storing the two larger bags under the bed he opened his briefcase.

It looked like a standard briefcase, but Oliver Blackwood had given this one to him, and it contained a false bottom. Thomas emptied the contents of the brief- case and then placed his thumb at the center and back of the case and applied pressure. A hidden spring re- leased and a small click went off. The bottom slid away, revealing a secret compartment that housed a 38 caliber Webley Mark IV standard issue British Army sidearm.

The gun barrel was thick and black and the blackish brown handle gave the weapon a powerful look. It was nudged in the case next to two boxes of ammunition.

The silence of the room was suddenly interrupted by the sound of screeching brakes and the unmistakable noise that emanates from an accident. Walking out onto the verandah, Thomas looked down at the scene below. A small truck had collided with a bicycle and a young lady lay bleeding on the ground. Several people were attempting to extricate the driver while others tended to the young lady. Who it appears was the unfortunate rider of the bicycle. Thomas remained for a few minutes watching the activity below. After he was satisfied that no one was seriously injured, he walked back into the hotel room.

Entering the room from the verandah Thomas stopped dead in his tracks. Franklyn had returned to the room and was holding a bottle of rum in one hand and caressing Thomas's gun, which still lay in the briefcase, with the other hand.

"What the devil are you doing, you little bastard?" Thomas yelled, crossing the room and snatching the briefcase from under Franklyn's hand. "You're nothing but a bloody little thief." He said, grabbing hold of Franklyn's wrist and wrenching it backwards.

Franklyn dropped the bottle of rum on the bed and twisting away from Thomas's grip responded in a shaky voice.

"I'm sorry, boss man, I just ain't never seen a gun like that before… it's beautiful."

"I've half a mind to thrash you to teach you not to touch other people's things," Thomas began, a little surprised by Franklyn's description of the gun as beautiful. He had never looked at a gun as beautiful before and he found it rather odd.

Thomas relaxed a little. He realized that he had screwed up leaving the case exposed, and this boy was just curious. Franklyn had crossed the room to get out of Thomas's reach and once he was sure the older man was not going to harm him he spoke.

"I ain't never seen no gun like that before boss. The only guns round here is the ones those soldiers carry on Hog Island."

"Soldiers, what soldiers? British soldiers?" asked Thomas.

"No they ain't British like you they is German soldiers who does speak like Mr. Wiegard."

Wiegard. Thomas knew the name and he knew that Wiegard was a Swiss industrialist living in these islands. Blackwood had prepared him as to who were the people of interest who lived in the Bahamas. But what was he doing with German soldiers and what was Hog Island?

"What is Hog Island and are you sure these men are German soldiers?"

Franklyn proceeded to tell Thomas a story about how Wiegard got the new Governor to clear off Hog Island and then about the night that he and his cousin Michael snuck back over to Hog Island and how Michael never came back and how he had heard a gunshot...

Thomas listened intently as Franklyn described the cave complex and all that was going on with the guards and the men in the white coats.

"So what reason did the authorities give your family for moving them off of Hog Island?" Thomas asked.

"They said something about Mr. Wiegard doing some experiments that could be dangerous but that it was all going to be good for this place."

Thomas opened the bottle of rum and pouring the brown liquor into a glass turned to Franklyn and said, "I want to see Hog Island as soon as possible."

CHAPTER TWENTY

Thursday, November 6th, 1941
One mile off of Hog Island

The channel between Nassau and Hog Island was about two miles wide and a strong current ran east to west and through Nassau Harbour. Thomas and Franklyn drifted in a small fifteen-foot Ketch with two fishing lines cast overboard. Neither man nor boy were interested in fishing and neither noticed when one of the lines received a bite. Thomas lay low in the hull of the Ketch and had a straw hat was pulled down low over his eyes. They had been scouting Hog Island all morning.

Franklyn directed Thomas's eyes to the southeastern side of Hog Island.

"You see those trees off the southern point of the island?"

"Yes, to the right of that big clump of bushes?" replied Thomas.

"Exactly," Franklyn said. "Through that cut you come up to a big dip in the land. It goes down and there are these caves down there. The stuff I been telling you about been going on down near them caves, dats where I seen dem German type soldiers and dem men in white coats."

"We are going to have to come back here at night," Thomas said. "Can you get us in close? I need to go ashore."

"I can get us right up to the shoreline. I know a little cut through them trees. We could slip right up to the land, I'll get you in there, boss man."

"Right, well let's pack up this gear and get back in," said Thomas. "It's getting late."

Franklyn quickly stowed the fishing gear away and turned the boat back toward Nassau Harbour. The small outboard engine sputtered and spat its way toward home. The trip back took about twenty minutes, and as they pulled up to the wharf Thomas could see Commissioner Atkinson pacing the dock.

"Good afternoon, Mr. Nash," Commissioner Atkinson said as Thomas threw him a mooring line.

"Good afternoon, Commissioner. All is well, I presume," Thomas called back.

"Quite," replied the Commissioner, tying the bowline to a wooden cleat on the dock.

Thomas scrambled out of the boat and onto the dock and came face to face with the Commissioner.

"Took a little ride around the harbour. The water is incredibly beautiful."

"Yes, well. I don't get out on the water as much as I used to but it still remains my favorite thing to do. Tell me Mr. Nash, did this young man take you over to Hog Island?" Commissioner Atkinson asked, nodding in Franklyn's direction.

"No, not at all," replied Thomas. "He did tell me about it, though. I understand that the whole island is off limits."

"That's correct. The government is involved with private enterprise which is conducting top-secret work with the intent of benefiting the local economy."

Thomas could not help himself from staring directly at the Commissioner as he spoke and he knew that the man had not spoken these words with any conviction.

"Well, that's good news for the locals I assume," said Thomas.

"Yes, hopefully it will result in jobs for the future," replied the Commissioner. "The purpose of my seeking you out is to invite you to join His Royal Highness tomorrow evening for a good, old-fashioned poker game."

"Tomorrow night, you say?"

"Yes, at eight o'clock at Government house."

"It will be my honor to be there," Thomas replied. "Thank you for inviting me."

"The invitation is from His Majesty himself. He was pleased to make your acquaintance the other day, I'm sure he will have many questions as to the home front."

"I look forward to a most pleasant evening," replied Thomas.

The commissioner excused himself and walked down the dock and back towards his car.

Thomas turned to Franklyn and glancing in the direction of Hog Island.

"We go tonight."

CHAPTER TWENTY-ONE

Friday, November 7th
2 a.m.
Nassau Harbour

Thomas and Franklyn waited until the darkest hour of the night before setting off toward Hog Island. Thomas lay low in the boat, dressed in a pair of black swim trunks and a dark green sweater. The sweater covered the gun that he had strapped to his waist. He also had a wool cap which he had pulled low over his head in an effort to hide his blonde hair. Franklyn was bare-chested and wearing a pair of raggedy shorts. Anyone who happened to look out over the harbour would figure that it was just a young man heading out for a night of fishing.

As the small boat approached Hog Island, Franklyn spoke in a soft whisper,

"Not long now, boss. I'm goanna put her right in between that cut directly up ahead, once we pass them two tall pine trees ain't nobody gonna be able to see this boat."

Thomas adjusted his seat and peered over the front of the boat toward the cut in the trees that Franklyn had indicated. He double-checked the firearm strapped to his side and sat patiently waiting for Franklyn to do his job.

The boy was an expert with the boat and he had cut the small engine and was using the natural current along with a single oar to guide the vessel silently between the two towering pine trees that grew out from the island's shore.

The boat glided between the trees and right up onto a small sand bar just ten feet from solid ground. Jumping out of the boat, Franklyn grabbed a rope and waded ashore.

Rolling himself out of the boat, Thomas's feet made a slight splash as they broke the surface. Scrambling quickly through the shin deep water, he followed Franklyn onto the beach.

Franklyn quickly fastened the rope to a tree and then scooted up next to Thomas who had ducked behind a thick set of bushes. Thomas looked around in an effort to gain his bearings.

"If we go right up that little ridge, past that tree line we got about a ten-minute walk to them caves I was telling you about," said Franklyn.

"Right," Thomas said in a hushed voice. "Lead on and let's try to make as little noise as possible."

Franklyn rose and started in the direction of the tree line. Thomas followed and slowly they made their way up the beach, past the tree line and into the interior of the island.

They had been hiking for about ten minutes when Franklyn stopped and motioned to Thomas to duck down behind some large rocks.

"If we go towards the east we gonna be able to come up on the caves from a little hill, that's the place I left Michael." Thomas heard the crack in Franklyn's voice at the mention of his cousin.

"Let's approach carefully," Thomas said. "You point the way but I'm going to take the lead."

Thomas could feel the ground sloping upward as the slowly walked toward the Eastern part of the Island. It was only a matter of minutes before they came up to the crest of the hill and suddenly a voice came clearly through the still night air.

"Gib mir eine Zigarette."

German.

Thomas could not believe his ears. *He was on a supposedly deserted island in the middle of nowhere with nothing around and someone was speaking German!*

Thomas changed his position so he could get a look down from his vantage point toward the direction of the voice and the smoke. Peering through the bushes from his hiding place he could see two guards with rifles standing in a clearing, smoking cigarettes. Beyond the clearing and on the other side of the guards Thomas could see a large rock formation and a low light emanating from what appeared to be an entrance carved out of the rocks.

Franklyn had managed to position himself next to Thomas and he whispered in his ear, "That's the entrance to the caves."

Thomas's mind was racing now. Germans were standing guard over a cave entrance on a deserted island in the Bahamas. *What the hell was in that cave and what the hell had he stumbled upon?*

He motioned for Franklyn to get closer and he whispered into the boy's ear.

"I need to get inside that cave. I want you to quietly work your way to the other side of the ravine and I need you to create a distraction."

Franklyn nodded his head in acknowledgment but Thomas could tell that the boy was perspiring and he grabbed his arm in an attempt to call him down.

For his part, Thomas's senses were on high alert and he had no doubt that his intensity was contributing to Franklyn's anxiety but he could not worry about any of that at this time.

"I'm going to give you ten minutes to get into place and then I want you to start making some noise. Howl like a wounded animal...cry out in pain... raise holy hell but get their attention I need those guards distracted long enough to get into that cave." Thomas looked the boy directly in the eyes as he spoke this was too crucial to screw up. "Do you understand me, lad?

Franklyn nodded his understanding.

"Now one last thing," Thomas continued. "You distract them for no more than three minutes and then you make your way back to the boat. Is that understood?"

"Three minutes?" Franklyn asked.

"Three minutes," Thomas repeated. "And then you get the hell back to the boat."

"But what about you, boss?"

Thomas cut him off. "Don't worry about me, I'll be there you just get the boat ready and I'll be there."

Franklyn nodded his head and then quietly slipped away from Thomas making his way around to the other side of the ridge.

Thomas slumped down behind the large rock formation and looked at his watch. The events of the past few months were all converging in his head and he knew he needed to clear his thoughts before attempting to get past those guards and into that cave. Who knew what was waiting for him on the other side? He knew he had to get inside those caves.

He ran his finger over his weapon expertly checking the gun and then looked at his watch again; two and a half minutes had passed.

What had Churchill roped him into? The old buzzard knew something was amiss with His Royal Highness, but what exactly was the old man's game? He was really on his own, a bizarre mission to try, judge and execute the Duke of Windsor and now there were Germans involved. Did Churchill have a clue, or was this all a set up designed to get him to assassinate Edward to serve some greater purpose?

Again, Thomas pushed these thoughts from his mind. They weren't the first time they had occurred to him but right now he needed to get into that cave and find out what the devil Edward was overseeing here in these islands. Somebody had to know these Germans were here.

In a moment, the stillness of the night was shattered with the most awful soul screeching sound Thomas had ever heard. Even though he was awaiting Franklyn's distraction, the noise startled him and after his initial reaction, he found himself tempted to laugh. He quickly gathered himself and carefully peered over the rock formation down to the area where the guards were stationed just as Franklyn let out another anguished wail.

The guards had moved away from Thomas's side of the ridge and were looking up to the tree line from where that screeching wails were emanating. Franklyn chimed in again with another blood curtailing cry and the guards started to move further away from the entrance to the cave. Thomas used the guard's movement as a cover for his own and made his move.

Using the terrain and Franklyn's screams as cover, Thomas bolted from behind the rock formation, down the ridge and into the clearing to the left of the cave opening. He quickly ducked inside the cave's mouth and out of the view of the guards.

He crouched down low hiding in what little shadow the entrance to the cave provided from the moonlight. He waited and controlled his breathing; so far, so good.

A distant glow of light came deep from a passageway through a downward sloping tunnel. Listening for any kind of noise or disturbance, he slowly and carefully withdrew his pistol and released the safety. The release of the safety made a short quick snap, which echoed in the cave and Thomas cursed himself for not anticipating that particular situation. He gathered himself up from his crouched position and slowly, while hugging the cave wall, made his way down the tunnel toward the light.

Moving deeper into the cave complex, the floor below him began to slope downward and the ceiling began to rise in parts. He kept close to the wall and in the shadows that were created by what little lighting was coming from up ahead.

As he approached a turn in the tunnel, he began to hear the sound of muffled voices. He crouched down and concentrated on the sound. More German! Muffled, but German.

He proceeded slowly and as the light began to get brighter the tunnel opened up into what seemed like a balcony overlooking large well-lit fully functioning laboratory.

Thomas quickly found a spot in the shadows from where he could observe everything. There were several people working. Two were dressed like the guards who were stationed outside and both held semiautomatic weapons strung from their shoulders. The others were all dressed in lab coats. On the far wall, set further back away from Thomas's position, appeared to be an assembly line of some sort.

Bunsen burners and glass tubing dominated one section of the oversized workbench and Thomas, who had failed chemistry twice in school, smiled at his ability to at least recognize the chemical equipment.

The German being spoken was barely audible and Thomas wished he had a better grasp of the language. That aside, he had stumbled across some secret German laboratory and he was going to have to figure out what the hell it all meant.

On the other side of the alcove, from where he had hidden himself, the stone terrace sloped downward to the floor below. He could go no further without risking exposure so he decided to get out and back to the boat. He had stayed too long and seen enough for the time being.

Rising slowly to his feet, Thomas adjusted his vision and started making his way back up the tunnel when the silence was shattered by a terrorizing savage scream. He quickly dropped back down into a squat position and scrambled back to his vantage point.

All of the labs occupants who were working diligently just a few moments ago were in a panic. They were scrambling in every direction and an older man in a white lab coat was barking out orders and trying to control the chaos.

"Beruhigen jetzt nach unten. Es gibt keine ausbreitung, gibt es keine ausbreitung," the man kept screaming in German.

Again Thomas cursed himself for his poor German but as best he could make out, the man was screaming to everyone to calm down and that there was no spread. He kept repeating the words "no spread, no spread," "Es gibt keine ausbreitung, gibt es keine ausbreitung"

The lab workers quickly gained their composure and as they calmed down, Thomas peered out from his hiding place and was struck by the most gruesome sight he could recall. One of the scientists lay dead on the ground next to the workbench holding the glass tubing and Bunsen burners. Thomas knew he was dead because the man had no face. Even from up above, he could see right through the man's eye socket to a mass of blood and skull.

The panic had been replaced by shock and as some of the workers began to look away, the older man spoke again but in a calmer and slower voice which aloud Thomas to comprehend the gist of his words.

"It was an accident," the older man said. "An accident, it is also a lesson that what we are doing is noble, but dangerous work. Accidents make us stronger."

The man's words seemed to have their desired effect and he continued to speak. "There was no spread. Hans was working with such a small amount of the compound that there was only enough to kill him and no one else. We need to continue to be careful, but now we must bury our Hans and learn the lesson that his death must teach us."

Thomas found himself staring at the hollowed out skull of the young aforementioned Hans. What the hell kind of chemical could eat a man's face away like that and that quickly?

Snapping back to attention, he quickly moved back up the tunnel and toward the cave entrance. The accident in the lab was the perfect cover for his exit.

He approached slowly trying to get a glimpse or idea where the two guards Franklyn had distracted were. He hoped the boy was all right and had done as he was told and gone back to the boat.

The guards were nowhere in sight. He moved quickly and exited the cave in a flash scooting away from the cave entrance and into the underbrush and pine trees. He didn't look back and just as quietly as possible made his way steadily away from the caves and up to the ridge above that would lead back to the boat.

As he reached the top of the ridge he knelt down in some bushes and paused to ascertain if the guards had re-appeared and if there was any activity whatsoever. Satisfied that he had made a clean get a way, he stood up and exited the bush and walked onto the well-worn path that Franklyn had brought him down earlier.

He sensed it at the last moment but wasn't quick enough to avoid the entire blow. The man came from his left and, with first-class rugby technique, tackled Thomas. The hit was a direct broadside and Thomas, along with his attacker, slammed violently into the ground.

He recovered quickly. Using his upper body strength, he rolled his assailant over and kicked out of the man's grasp. The reprieve was brief as the attacker had drawn a knife and was now lunging at him.

Thomas timed his move perfectly and as the attacker lunged forward with the out stretched knife, he pivoted on his back foot, and grabbed the man's arm as it thrust by.

His attacker countered and he expertly dropped to the ground and spun around, sweeping Thomas's feet from under him and sending both men crashing hard to the ground.

The attacker recovered faster and pounced on Thomas, who had got himself caught in some of the un-derbrush and that's when he felt the knife rip across his right forearm.

The pain was searing, both hot and cold at the same time but Thomas knew he had precious little time before this assailant was on him again. The man was on top now, raining down blows on his head. Thomas desperately felt around for any type of weapon and his right hand found a palm-sized rock. He held off his attacker's blows with his left hand and started to bring the rock forward to strike him when the assailant slammed his fist into Thomas's jaw knocking him out cold.

CHAPTER TWENTY-TWO

Thursday, November 6ᵗʰ
3:30 p.m.
Wiegard Residence
Nassau, Bahamas

Wiegard listened pensively as Krueger relayed the events of the intruder on Hog Island as well as the chemical accident that killed the young scientist, Hans.

"I have him tied up in the back of the cave," Krueger said, "His British Government issued identification card says his name is Thomas Nash and that he is with the agriculture department. Ever heard of him?"

"No," Wiegard replied. "From what you tell me, I can assure you he is not an agriculturist. Haven't you interrogated him?"

" He was still out cold when I left to come and report to you. But don't worry, I'm going back to have a little chat with him tonight."

"The chemicals," Wiegard began. "They're more dangerous than we previously thought. I was not fully aware of how powerful until this trip. I want you to review all the protocols used in the lab. We cannot afford another accident. We cannot allow doubt or fear to enter into the minds of those scientists – this project must be finished."

"I understand," Krueger said. "I will double-check everything."

Wiegard was exhausted having travelled nonstop since his meeting with Hitler. As soon as he had landed back in Nassau, He had sent for Wallis. He had a note hand delivered to her demanding she be at his home in the next two hours, no excuses. He would not allow this 'Thomas Nash agriculturist' or the accident to dampen his spirits. Hitler himself had anointed him and now he wanted his reward.

Turning back to Krueger he said, "I have given the entire staff the afternoon off. I am having a visitor. I would like you alone to remain here. You can go back to Hog Island tonight and have your conversation with this Mr. Nash then."

"Yes sir," Krueger said. "I'll make sure the staff has cleared out and that everything is secure."

"Good. I expect a full report on this Mr. Nash in the morning. Now let me be."

As Krueger left to attend to his duties, Wiegard unpacked a large white box that contained a gift from Hitler to Edward. Today He would give it to Wallis to give to Edward.

The house was quiet and the weather was perfect. It was unusual for this time of year because Nassau was known to be very hot and humid in September.

Wallis arrived promptly at four o' clock having driven in one of the older Government house vehicles that she and Edward used to drive around the island on Sunday afternoons. She had, of course, been to Wiegard's home several times for parties and social gatherings but this would be only the second time she would visit his home alone. Their affair had been conducted mainly aboard his sailing sloop and more often than not inside Government House itself. Their lovemaking was always so desperate, bordering on the violent, but Wiegard had learned how to handle and please her.

He had learned that a strong, dominant woman like Wallis could only respond to an even stronger more dominant man. Wiegard was still a little surprised at how rough and tumble Wallis was in bed and at times he thought he was actually hurting her when she demanded that he be even harsher.

Wiegard opened the door to greet the Duchess. She was dressed, as always, with outstanding attention to detail: in a custom tailored light coral suit, holding a small white purse in her hand. Her hair was pulled straight back in her customary fashion and her lips were painted a ripe ruby red. Her face showed no emotion when Wiegard opened the door. He realized that she was angry, or pretending to be. Wiegard extended her his hand and after a moment's pause, she accepted it with a bit of reluctance. With a single swift powerful motion he pulled her toward him and the force drew her into his arms and into his foyer. He slammed the door behind her and engulfed her in a grand embrace.

Wallis at first stiffened in resistance but Wiegard was a powerful man and her resistance to him evaporated. Picking her up, he carried her like a new bride up the winding staircase, which sat just off the foyer, and threw her onto the large bed in his master bedroom.

Wallis landed on the bed with a bounce and as she adjusted to face Wiegard she spoke.

"Allow me to remove my dress before you ruin it and I have to explain what happened."

Wiegard grunted in impatience and stepped back. Wallis slipped of the bed and then expertly disrobed. It was more than Wiegard could handle and as she turned to him in just her slip and undergarments, he pounced.

They're lovemaking was raw and vigorous and Wiegard possessed her with a ferocity that even surprised him. He still did not understand the depth of the effect she had on him and as always, after their physical encounter, he was left drained. It was in these moments that Wiegard could begin to understand why Edward had given up the throne. Wallace could possess and control a man like no other woman Wiegard had ever known.

As they lay on the big linen sheeted bed, exhausted from their lovemaking and with the afternoon sun's light dancing off the trees outside the master bedroom, Wallis sat up in the bed and spoke.

"I am still angry with you Rolf. How dare you disappear for two weeks with out telling me?"

Wiegard, flat on his back, looked up at her. He was amused that after their rough and tumble exchange her lipstick and makeup were still perfect.

"It was unavoidable," he said. "I was summoned and it was for a meeting of the highest caliber."

"The highest caliber? What strange and secretive language you use. Are you attempting to impress me? If so, rest assured I am not impressed."

Wiegard sat up in the bed and reached over to the nightstand retrieving a cigarette. After lighting it and drawing the smoke deep into his lungs, he exhaled and watched the smoke billow against the ceiling over the bed.

"Would you be impressed if I told you that I met with the great man himself and that he asked about you and we discussed your little plan to kidnap the Royal Princesses?" Wiegard said, taking another drag off of the cigarette.

"You mean you met with Hitler? You were summoned by Hitler himself and he asked about me?"

"Yes."

"Well, what did he say? What did he want to know?"

Wiegard rose from the bed and walked over to the other side of the room and wrapped himself in a robe that had been laid across the sofa. He then proceeded to the closet and retrieved the large white box he had stored there earlier.

"Is that for me? Is it from Hitler himself?"

"No," replied Wiegard. "Not everything is about you. This is for Edward and I want you to give it to him."

Wiegard proceeded to untie the black chord that was wrapped around the box and opened it on the bed next to Wallis. The Duchess removed the tissue paper and pressed and folded neatly was the overcoat and uniform, including the cap, of a German Grand Admiral.

"This is the uniform that Hitler wants Edward to wear when you return to Britain. His majesty will be King of the British people but he will hold the rank of Grand Admiral in the German Navy. He will owe his throne to Hitler. Look there on the cap, you see how the swastika is positioned on top of the British Royal Coat of arms."

He sat down on the sofa enjoying the little drama he was playing out with Wallis. He looked back at her sitting up in the bed with the sheets pulled up around her neck in an effort to cover her nakedness.

"It's a lovely costume," Wallis said, sarcasm seeping into her words. "But I fail to see how having a beautiful uniform returns us to power?"

Wiegard finished smoking the cigarette and stumped it out in an ashtray that lay on a small end table next to the sofa. He looked back at Wallis.

"The Fuhrer summoned me to Germany to meet with him and his naval commanders to discuss the installation and implementation of my catapult launch mechanism. He shared with me his plans for the future."

"I don't have a clue what a catapult whatever it is, as you call it is and how any of this relates to me," said Wallis, her irritation becoming more open.

"Patience, my dear," replied Wiegard. "All will be explained in time."

He rose from the sofa and walked to the large bay window that overlooked the beach and the water at the back of his property. With his back toward Wallis he continued.

"As you know, we have been conducting some experiments on Hog Island. Experiments with chemicals, specifically a chemical component that can be attached to a rocket and using my catapult mechanism, or whatever it is, as you call it, this chemical rocket can be launched from a U-boat."

Wiegard turned to face Wallis but her expression was unchanged. He was not sure if she didn't quite understand or if she was just masking her comprehension of what he had just told her. Wallis, for her part, was sitting cross-armed waiting for him to continue.

"Well, the Fuhrer summoned me to congratulate me on my design and on the progress we have made on Hog Island," Wiegard said, resuming his seat on the sofa.

Wallis stared at him for a long moment and then spoke.

"That's it! I already knew about your chemical experiment on Hog Island and you have been telling me for over a year now about plans to restore us to the throne. How does any of this have to do with accomplishing that and what did Hitler say about me?"

"It has everything to do with you and restoring Edward to the throne," he replied, growing irritated with Wallis's sense of entitlement. Did she not understand what a huge accomplishment it was for him to be recognized by Hitler?

"Because of me, this war will end sooner than later and because of me, America will be brought to her knees and will be forced to bow to Hitler himself," Wiegard said, his voice rising in irritation.

"And what exactly is it that you are going to do to bring all of this about?" ;Her tone matching his.

"What I am going to do is make damn sure that my catapult system and my chemical rocket perform as they are designed to perform and by Christmas of this year the American Government will lay in ruins. Britain, without America's help, will have no choice but to surrender and you and your Duke will ascend the throne as Herr Hitler will look to you and Edward to win the peace with the British people."

Wallis stared at Wiegard intently for a few moments before beginning to laugh.

At first Wiegard was confused but then as Wallis's laughter grew louder and more animated he started to get angry.

"What is it that so amuses you?" His teeth clenched.

"You, you amuse me," she replied, continuing to laugh. "You are sitting here wrapped in a cloth robe talking about how because of you America will be brought to her knees, because of you Britain will fall." She bobbed her head back and forth. "Can you not appreciate how silly that sounds coming from a half-naked man stuck on a pimple of an island in the middle of nowhere? America – do you have any idea how vast and great America is! Do you really think your little rocket and your little catapult can bring down America?"

Wiegard was growing angrier by the moment. Who did this pretentious shrew think she was? She was nobody a piece of flesh, a piece of meat. To be used and discarded just as she used and discarded people. Did she not know who he was? How brilliant his mind was? What he had accomplished? Hitler knew. Because of him, America would be neutralized.

It was this thought that caused him to regain control. Wallis had stopped laughing now. She had become aware that he was not laughing and her face betrayed her realization that he was angry.

"Rolf. Don't be upset with me, I'm just a little frustrated and I don't understand."

Wiegard did not change expression but he answered her trying to inject some warmth into his words.

"It's alright, my dear. I can understand your frustration. You don't have all the facts and you can't quite see the role you will play."

He was aroused again but this time it was different. She had offended and mocked him and he was going to make her pay for it. He rose from the sofa and as he approached her he disrobed. A momentary flash of fear crossed her eyes as Wallis herself sensed a change in Wiegard.

"Tell me the role I'm to play," she said, pulling the covers up as if to afford some protection.

Wiegard swept the covers away and mounted the bed. His mouth was hot and his breathing deep as he enveloped her in his embrace. Wiegard did not hold back and as he roughly entered her and as he began to thrust at her he spoke in a low voice into her ear.

"You doubt me and you treat me like all of the other men you have had in your life, but my dear I am different from all of the men you have had. I am one of the chosen ones. One chosen by the Fuhrer himself to bring his great vision of the world to reality."

Any resistance on her part evaporated and Wiegard's lesson begun.

Krueger sat stunned in the room directly below Wiegard's bedroom. He had been there for the last two hours listening intently to all that had transpired between Wiegard and Wallis. Wiegard was part of Hitler's plans to attack the United States and based on all that was being discussed in the room above him, the attack was going to be devastating and tragic.

He had placed listening equipment in Wiegard's bedroom and at this moment he had heard more that he expected. It wasn't necessary for him to listen in on their second round of lovemaking, so he exited the room and decided to enter Wiegard's private office again and see if he could find the blueprints for the hydraulic launch system that the head scientist Karl had told him about. He had gotten into the office previously when Wiegard was out of town but had found nothing with regards to the blueprints. All Krueger found was a stack of leather journals that, after examination, revealed what Krueger already knew – namely that Wiegard was a meticulous man when it came to recording his daily schedule and events. He had witnessed Wiegard's dedication to his journal from the day he arrived and while in his private office had peeked into some of the journals.

His previous review of Wiegard's journals confirmed the existence of the catapult system but no clue as to blueprints or specifications. The journals also documented the affair Wiegard was conducting with Wallis. Krueger thought it a bit unusual and out of character for Wiegard to be so careless but nevertheless, every man had his Achilles heel.

He entered the office after picking the lock and making sure not to leave any scratches to indicate the unauthorized entry. A quick look around revealed that nothing was new from the last time he was in the office except for a new leather journal book that was sitting open on the desk. Krueger quickly crossed over to the desk and started to read Wiegard's latest entries into the journal.

What he saw on those pages confirmed what Wiegard had told Wallis about his trip to Germany, but halfway down the notes revealed the specifics and Krueger shook his head in disbelief.

The Japanese were going to attack Pearl Harbor and they were going to do it in a month's time, on December 7th. The same day Wiegard's chemical bombs were to be launched on Washington and New York.

He quickly re-positioned the journal exactly as he had found it and then exited Wiegard's office. After making sure that no one was around, he stepped out back to have a smoke and think. He wanted to be true to his real mission but the information that he now possessed was overwhelming and he needed time to think.

Deciding it was time to have a little talk with the tied-up Thomas Nash, Krueger boarded one of the small launches and headed back to Hog Island.

CHAPTER TWENTY-THREE

June 6th, 2013
Katherine Blackwood's sitting room

"Pearl Harbor," Nicholas began, and then stopped.

"Go on," Katherine said, prodding him.

"Wiegard's journal documents the joint planning by Germany and Japan, a double-hit, but only Pearl Harbor was attacked. Was there any other evidence presented to suggest that this plot or coordinated effort ever took place?"

"No," came Katherine's sharp reply. "The only evidence is Wiegard's diary and what transpired next."

Nicholas met her gaze and opened his mouth to speak but then restrained himself from blurting out what was on the tip of his tongue.

"The answer to your question," Katherine continued, "is yes. I have Wiegard's Journals."

Nicholas slumped back in his seat letting it all run through his mind. "Wow."

After a few more minutes of contemplation, Nicholas looked at Katherine and said," It's unbelievable. So many lives lost at Pearl Harbor and so many more that could have been killed by the Hog Island weapons, my God, did we really come that close to losing the war?"

"Yes, we did," Katherine replied. "But courageous men prevailed and only Pearl Harbor was struck."

"Courageous men," Nicholas repeated.

"Nash, from the highest level, licensed to kill, if you will allow for the James Bond reference, and prepared to right the evils of the world. These men, who operate so far outside the law, become the only real justice left in the world. They right those things that the laws and the courts cannot or will not."

Katherine shifted in her chair before continuing. "We have spoken before about honor and service and men like Nash, men who perform these services sometimes for the government and sometimes for the prime minister as in the case of Thomas Nash, and in the case of your father," Katherine paused and looked directly at Nicholas. "At the behest of the Monarch."

Nicholas stared at Katherine who remained motionless in her chair waiting for his response.

After a few silent moments he asked, "You mean the Queen, Elizabeth the second? The current Queen?"

"That is correct. Elizabeth the second, the reigning monarch, and the same monarch who was sitting on the throne in 1997, the year your father never returned."

Nicholas rubbed his jaw and bent his head forward, looking through the top of his eyes at Katherine. His expression told her to continue.

"Your father was one of those unheralded saviors of our great nation and he was a man who could be counted on to know the right thing to do and to have the strength to do it even when the act itself was morally reprehensible. You see, your father was a sin eater. Those souls, who take the sins of the world upon themselves, leaving the rest of us to live out our lives in ignorant bliss," Katherine sat up straight and fixed her gaze directly at Nicholas. "Some people would condemn your father, and other men like him, for the things that they have done, but they would be ignorant of the truth. Prior to this evening, I would venture to guess that you would be one of those types of people."

"You would have been correct," Nicholas replied in a subdued tone. "But that was prior to this evening."

Katherine smiled and the softness of it seemed to give Nicholas some sense of warmth. He hesitated for a few moments. "Do you know what happened to him and why he never came home?" He could tell that she was deep in her thoughts but she looked directly at him and said,

"I do, but I will, for now, only speak in generalities. You will know the true story of your father's life and death before we are through and then," she paused and allowed that wry smile to cross her lips again, "you will have a decision to make."

Nicholas wondered what decision might be, but he put that thought out of his mind for the time being.

Katherine continued, her voice growing stronger and more animated.

"Your father succeeded in his mission where Nash never did. Edward lived, but the ironic thing is that both missions were the same mission – just separated by the span of 56 years.

Your father and Nash were both ordered to dish out judgment to traitors and justice for Great Britain and at the request of the highest authority. Your father was a great man whose service saved our very way of life. He goes unheralded, at the very least, you his son will know the truth and I know that you will guard it and understand that he was a man of honor and a man of service to the crown."

Nicholas had listened intently and he sensed that Katherine was invigorated. He noted that every time she spoke of Andrew Stone she was more animated. It was obvious that she had deeply loved his father.

Katherine rose from her seat. It was well past 11, but she showed no sign of stopping. "Come on," she said, picking up the teapot. "I'm going to make us a fresh pot and I want to show you a very special place, a place where your father spent hours in solitude and contentment."

Rising from his seat and following Katherine into the kitchen, Nicholas searched his thought for some sense of order to all that he was learning. Everything he thought he knew was changing and yet somehow he welcomed it.

CHAPTER TWENTY-FOUR

Friday, November 7th
1 a.m.
Hog Island

Thomas slowly opened his eyes. He had regained consciousness for some time now but continued to play possum while he took in his surroundings. He was tied up and face down on a cold, stone floor. It was dark and damp and he could hear the muffled voices of the German scientist off in the distance. He was alone, probably somewhere deep in the cave complex.

His head was sore and his throat as dry as the sand that ringed the island. Very little light penetrate where he was but off to his left he could make out a covered mound whose odor identified it as a dead body. A smell he was all too familiar with from his days in France.

Thomas's eyes were just beginning to adjust when he heard the sounds of approaching footsteps. A bright torchlight broke the darkness and he kept his eyes closed.

"Open your eyes Mr. Nash," a voice from behind the torchlight spoke out. "I know you are awake, I've been watching you for sometime."

Thomas slowly opened his eyes and started to speak but the dryness of his throat caused him to cough. He swallowed hard and then forced himself up and into a sitting position, his hands still tied behind his back.

The voice behind the torchlight spoke up. "My name is Manfred Krueger and I would like to ask you, Mr. Nash, what are you doing on my island?"

"Your island? Thomas replied in a raspy voice. "The last time I checked this island was the property of the British Empire, you Nazi pig."

Thomas watched as Krueger turn off the light; remove a large radio from his belt placing it next to himself as he sat down in a folding chair directly across from him.

"I'm actually an American of German heritage, but if it helps you to identify me as a Nazi, go ahead. I still want to know what the hell you are doing snooping around Hog Island?"

"So you're an American Nazi," Thomas said. "Makes no difference to me. You're still scum."

Thomas watched the smile spread across Krueger's face. "You're pretty spunky for an agriculturist. I would have expected a more, shall we say, less combative personality."

Thomas turned his head to one side and spat the dried contents of his mouth out on the floor of the cave.

"I'll give you a sip of water if you answer my question," Krueger said, pulling a small metal canteen from his back pocket. "What are you doing on Hog Island?"

Thomas locked eyes with Krueger and both men continued to stare at each other for a few minutes.

"All right then," Krueger said, rising to his feet. "Let me show you something, Mr. Nash," Walking over to the covered mound to the left of him, Krueger ripped the tarp off uncovering the mound. Krueger knelt down and reaching over the mound pulled the body of the dead scientist Hans to an up right sitting position the eaten out face and head slumped to one side.

Thomas was grateful for the dark, but even in that poor light he could see the grotesqueness of the scientist's missing face.

Thomas began to laugh. Krueger let Hans's body go and the corpse slumped back down to the ground. "I'm glad that this amuses you so much," Krueger said, rising to his feet, "I assure you that if you do not answer my questions, it won't be so amusing."

"I don't scare easily, Mr. Krueger," Thomas replied. "Your little chemical accident here does not frighten me."

"It should. I heard that his screams were so terrible that God himself wept."

Thomas smiled again. "Me thinks you have a flair for the dramatic."

Krueger began to speak when one of the guards came rushing in. "Mr. Krueger, Mr. Krueger, come quickly sir, something has happened."

Krueger immediately got to his feet and both he and the guard rushed back towards the laboratory area.

Thomas called out as they retreated. "Nice chatting with you Mr. Krueger. Hope we can do it again some-time, provided you don't blow yourself and all of the rest of your Nazi scum to high heaven. You bloody bastards."

Thomas broke into a horrible hacking cough and his throat was as raw as a piece of meat fresh from the kill.

As his coughing subsided, he thought he heard a noise. Quickly getting control of his cough he held his breath and listened intently.

"Boss, boss," a muffled voice called out.

Thomas cocked his head to one side and he heard it again but this time he could tell it was coming from above him. He looked up from his position on the floor and there climbing down from the ceiling was Franklyn.

The boy looked like a pirate, He was skinning a large tree vine that dealt as a rope and he had a knife gripped between his teeth as he descended.

Franklyn landed softly on the cave floor and removed the knife from his mouth. He quickly moved towards Thomas and cut the bindings that had tied his hands.

Rubbing his wrists from where the ties had cut him he whispered to Franklyn, "How boy, how did you get in here?"

"From up above," Franklyn replied, grinning. "These caves they got a ceiling and up above this one is some rocks that hide a small hole that does drop down right into this cave."

"But how did you know where they had me?" Thomas asked as he grabbed the large radio that Krueger had left on the cave floor."

"When you didn't make it to the boat, I came back looking for you," Franklyn replied, in a hushed voice. "That's when I saw that man that was talking to you just now drag you into the caves. I knew they would bring you to the back of the caves and I knows about this secret entrance from up top from my cousin Michael."

"Can we both get out on that vine?" Thomas asked indicating the clump of vine that Franklyn had climbed down on.

"Yeah it can handle us both, tree vine is strong," Franklyn replied.

Thomas looked around quickly just to make sure no one was approaching. "Right, hurry up then," he began. "You go first and I'll follow."

Thomas grabbed ahold of the vine and turned to hand it to Franklyn. The boy was frozen in his place and Thomas realized Franklyn was starring at Hans's burnt-out face.

"Franklyn," Thomas said, in a whisper. "Franklyn," he repeated. "Get a grip lad, now is not the time."

Franklyn didn't move so Thomas grabbed him from behind and spun him around slapping him rapidly across the face. The slap had its desired affect and Franklyn's trance was broken.

"We'll discuss it when we get out of here," Thomas said. "But right now we need to get out of here, so let's move."

Franklyn snapped into action and as nimbly grabbed hold of the vine and stared climbing up to the ceiling. Thomas held the vine taught giving Franklyn some added assistance and then shoving Krueger's radio in his pocket, climbed the vine himself.

Thomas reached the top of the cave and pulled himself up through a small break in the rocks that led to the outside. Once extricated from the cave, he filled his lungs with fresh air. They paused for only a few minutes to catch their breath and then Franklyn stood up and said, "This way boss, I got the boat close by."

CHAPTER TWENTY-FIVE

November 7th, 1941
6:45 p.m.
Shelborne Hotel, Miami Beach, Florida

Oliver Blackwood opened the double-French door leading out to the balcony of his suite overlooking Miami Beach. Jonathan Hanson already had a drink in his hand and was taking in the view of the skyline and the sun, which had just begun to set.

Blackwood joined his longtime friend on the balcony and both men stood in silence, marveling at the beauty of the sun slipping silently away for the day.

Hanson, from Boston, was one of the wealthiest men in the United States, if not the world, but unlike another wealthy Bostonian, Joe Kennedy, Hanson preferred to play it low key. Blackwood knew he was one of Hanson's true confidants and probably his only friend.

In the intelligence game, it was useful to have a contact like Hanson whose multimillion-dollar companies spanned the world and offered an effective cover from under which Blackwood operated.

The price for this cover that allowed Blackwood to move seamlessly through one world to another was that Jonathan Hanson made money every time.

Sometimes it was information, other times the takeover of a business or property that the owner had abandoned due in no small part to the world within which Blackwood operated. In all cases, Hanson made money.

Over the years, the relationship had served both men well and they had forged a friendship built on a deep trust in a game in which you could trust no one.

The only thing Hanson loved more than money was his only daughter, Nancy. Her marriage to David Atkinson and subsequent move to the Bahamas as the Commissioner's wife had to be sanctioned by Blackwood before Hanson would allow his daughter to become Atkinson's wife. Nancy's mother had died giving birth to her, and Jonathan Hanson had no other family. Blackwood recognized Hanson's independent streak in his daughter and convincing his good friend that his daughter was a chip of the old block, led Hanson to decide it was better to gain a son-in-law than lose a daughter.

It was true that the commissioner was fifteen years older than Nancy but he was a known commodity to Blackwood, their paths having crossed professionally during the Boar Wars and during younger days. Oliver Blackwood had no qualms in convincing Jonathan Hanson as to the merits of Commissioner David Atkinson.

That had been some seven years ago and Blackwood found himself almost as excited about Nancy's pending arrival as her father. He had after all, due to his frequent visits with her father, watched Nancy grow from a toddler to the beautiful woman she was today and he too felt a sense of parental care for her.

"I must say, Jonathan, I'm intrigued after all of these years that you would want to partake personally in the dirty side of our business."

"Are you asking me a question or just intrigued by it?" Hanson replied.

"No, I would rather try to figure it out on my own, a puzzle to solve, if you will," Blackwood said, smiling at his old friend. "In all these years you have never once asked to go operational, to get your hands dirty. For some reason, and I will figure out what that reason is, you asked to go on this one."

"I'll save you the trouble," Hanson said, looking at his watch, "Nancy is the only heir I have. Her plane lands in ten minutes and the time has come for her to learn the ways of the world or at least the world she will inherit. Besides," he said laughing, "I figured at our advanced age this probably was the last best chance I had of going on one of these."

Oliver Blackwood laughed at his friend's earnestness but he still thought it an odd request. "Don't get your hopes up for anything too dramatic," he said. "These things usually are routine. It's a good plan and Nancy is an excellent sailor. I must admit, when you said you wanted in you made things easier. You and Nancy can sail the yacht in to Nassau from Miami as simple as pie and I will be able to slip in and do what I have to do."

Jonathan Hanson grunted his approval. "Come on," he said, opening the door back into the hotel suite. "Let's go down to the bar and have a drink while we are waiting for Nancy. I can't wait to tell her how much money we're going to make."

CHAPTER TWENTY-SIX

Friday, November 7th, 1941
8 p.m.
Government House

It had been 18 hours since Thomas and Franklyn had returned from Hog Island and he had grilled the boy mercilessly about the caves, the natural harbour on the northern side and all about the locals being forced off of the island after Edward's arrival.

He had tried to get a little sleep earlier in the afternoon but to no avail, his mind would not let him be. His thoughts were racing even at this hour as he proceeded to climb the steps to the front entrance of Government House.

In a matter of moments, and for the second time, he was going to come face-to-face with His Royal Highness, the Duke of Windsor, Governor General of the Bahamas, a man he was charged with judging and if need be, executing. The absurdity of that thought and whatever it was he had stumbled into made him regret even more his lack of sleep; after all, he was going to need to be sharp going into this poker game.

Thomas reached the top of the stone steps that led up from the street in front of the Governor's mansion and he adjusted his tie before knocking of the front door. He had worn an old school blazer that he knew would elicit a comment from either the Duke or the Commissioner and he had carefully bandaged his right arm where his assailant had slashed during the fight on Hog Island. He had treated the wound by pouring whiskey on it to sanitize it and then he applied a tight bandage so as to control the bleeding. The bleeding had stopped, but as he reached for the doorknocker he felt the pain in his arm again and it reminded him of the strangeness of the day.

A tall black man dressed in black pants and a white dinner jacket almost immediately opened the door.

"Good evening, sir," the butler said. "Welcome to Government House."

"Thank you."

The butler stepped aside, allowing Thomas to enter the foyer, and then closed the door behind him.

"This way, please."

Thomas followed the butler down the hall way and into a large room off to the right. Walking through the house he noticed the portraits of both Edward and Wallis that hung in the hallway and could not help being irritated by their existence. How ridiculous, he thought, to feel the need to display one's own portrait as if one would forget who they were.

The room the butler led him into was very long and seemed to Thomas to run the entire side of the house. It had several sitting areas and the furnishings were a mixture of light rattan chairs and sofas as well as deep red velvet sofa. Thomas thought this sofa seemed out of place.

It was a well-lit room and on the light yellow walls hung portraits and pictures. At the far end of the room a card table had been set up and Commissioner Atkinson was standing and staring out of a side window with a drink in his hand.

"Mr. Nash," announced the butler. Thomas realized the butler knew his name.

Commissioner Atkinson turned to face Thomas.

"Good of you to be on time Nash." Crossing the room and offering his hand, the Commissioner continued. "What the devil happened to your face, man?"

"I fell down into some bushes while I was scouting some land for farming on the west side of the island."

"Well, it looks worse than that," the Commissioner said. "It looks as if you got beat to hell."

"I've had worse," Thomas replied.

"May I get the gentleman a cocktail?" The butler asked, interrupting their conversation.

"Yes, thank you. Whiskey neat."

"Very good sir."

"His Royal Highness is not down yet and we are also waiting on Mr. Wiegard who will be making up our fourth player. Have you met Wiegard yet? Asked the Commissioner.

"I have not had the pleasure," Thomas replied.

"Well, he is a very interesting chap. He is the fellow we shut down Hog Island for. I do not know exactly the nature of his work but he has promised that whatever he is doing over on Hog Island will lead to some local jobs and is supposed to be very good for the local economy."

Thomas was about to answer when the butler announced from the other side of the room.

"His Royal Highness."

Thomas turned in the direction of the Butler's voice and put his eyes on Edward.

The Governor General stood in the doorway of the grand room, as if waiting for a trumpeter to announce his entrance. He was dressed in a pair of grey trousers and a blue blazer with a green ascot tied around his neck. His shirt was pink and Thomas was struck by the fact that this somehow added to Edward's aloofness. His Majesty appeared, above it all, in fact Edward's eyes were looking directly through Thomas as if he were not there.

Commissioner Atkinson stepping forward and addressing Edward broke the moment.

"Good evening, your Majesty."

"Good evening, Commissioner," Edward replied.

Commissioner Atkinson cleared his throat and said. "I believe you have already met Mr. Thomas Nash. As your Highness knows, Mr. Nash has been sent to help increase our citrus production in our efforts to do what we can to support our fellow countrymen in the struggle."

Edward directed his attention towards Thomas.

"Your Majesty," said Thomas, as he instinctively bowed his head just a nod. Edward had not extended his hand and Thomas kept both of his clasped behind his back.

"Welcome to Government House Mr. Nash," Edward said. "What do you think of our little island?"

"It is quite charming and peaceful a place, but I have not had enough time to really get into any of the local customs."

"I daresay there are not many local customs worthy of getting into," Edward replied, as he lit a cigarette. "This colony is devoid of any civilized customs and that is precisely why we have this poker game, it keeps our spirits up and reminds us that even in the depths of isolation there is some civility in the world."

The butler had served Edward a drink and His Royal Highness moved over to sit on one of the rattan sofas.

He indicated to both Thomas and the commissioner to take a seat.

"We are waiting for Wiegard we assume?" Edward said exhaling.

"Yes your majesty, he will be making up the fourth this evening," replied the Commissioner.

"Is your wife not joining us tonight?"

"No sir, she is actually off the island and visiting her father. Some family business seems to have arisen."

"Pity, Wallis will be very disappointed. She will not have anyone to gossip with," Edward said, as he took a long drink from his glass and setting it down on the small coffee table.

He lit another cigarette before turning to Thomas.

"So tell us Mr. Nash, what did you do in this war to earn yourself banishment to our island?"

"Well sir, I was pretty banged up after Dunkirk and His Majesty's Government determined that I was no longer fit for active service and since I was a farmer before the war, well they sent me here to work on increasing the pineapple production in these islands."

"You were evacuated at Dunkirk?" Asked Edward.

"Yes sir," replied Thomas.

"Why do you think the Germans spared the British army that day Mr. Nash?"

"I am not sure they did spare us that day, Your Highness. The British people saved the day."

Edward leaned forward in his chair "Poppycock!" His voice rising. "The Germans could have annihilated the entire British Expeditionary Force that day but they allowed the army to be evacuated. Think man! Why?"

Edward had suddenly become very animated and Commissioner Atkinson shifted uncomfortably in his seat.

"The Germans could have strafed that beach a thousand times over but they did not and if you have not realized why, do not fret, you are after all just a simple man, a farmer as you say, but we are going to enlighten you." Edward spat out these last words.

Thomas felt the bile in him rising and he forced himself to stay calm though his mind was racing. This Edward was very different from the one who greeted him on the street jut a few days ago. This Edward was condescending this Edward would be easy to kill.

"Please continue, your majesty. Enlighten me," Thomas said, in as calm a voice as he could muster.

"Hitler wanted the British Army to survive," Edward said, whispering the words in exasperation. "Do you not see that the natural course, the best course, is one in which the superior survives. Hitler knows this and he knows that the Anglo Saxon is the superior man, he also knows what I know and that is that Britain is on the wrong side of this war."

This was an incredible statement to make. Edward was saying out loud things that were in direct opposition to his country and Thomas could sense the Commissioner's unease.

The Commissioner took a long drink from his glass and Thomas leaned forward and with great self-control addressed Edward.

"Surely your Majesty is not suggesting that Herr Hitler's way is the way for Britain?"

"We are suggesting that Her Hitler is correct in that a superior people are destined to rule the world and the reason he spared the British Army is because he knows that our two countries would be stronger if we joined together to fight the bloody scourge of communism. Why destroy an army that can be useful to you in the true struggle?"

Thomas could not believe his ears. Maybe Churchill was right, he thought, maybe Edward was a turncoat.

"Hess!" Edward exclaimed. "Six months ago the Deputy Fuhrer parachutes into Scotland with an offer of peace and prosperity and my brother's government, under Mr. Churchill does not embrace the common sense plan presented by Hitler to end this war, save countless British lives and guarantee that Britain and Germany rule the world." Sitting forward in his seat, Edward continued. "No, instead they imprison the man and hide him from the world. We have fools as leaders who lack vision. Vision to see that the real enemy is the Soviet. Communism is the devil incarnate to our way of life and Britain is doomed if the right leaders do not emerge."

Sitting back in his chair, Edward inhaled deeply on his cigarette.

Thomas sat back in his chair as well and concentrated on his breathing. His temper was flaring and his thoughts flashed back to his striking General Anderson after Dunkirk. He knew that he had to control himself better in this situation but it was proving to be difficult.

"Mr. Wiegard," announced the Butler and Rolf Wiegard entered the room as if he were boarding a yacht. He swept in and circled the entire room before presenting himself to Edward.

"Good evening your Majesty, you are looking fit."

Wiegard's entrance had broken the pall over the room and the tension that was building between Edward and Thomas.

"Good evening Herr Wiegard," replied Edward.

Thomas's mind snapped! And at that moment, he pronounced Edward guilty.

It was the greeting, Edward using the title, 'Herr' to address Wiegard. He knew it was the correct and polite salutation but Edward enjoyed saying it too much. A small but telling sign, Edward was already thinking as a German.

Thomas knew, at that moment, he was going to kill Edward. He had slapped General Anderson because of his gross incompetence and had railed against a system of promotion by social status and birth right, and this banished King, was just the same old thing but at an even more treacherous and nefarious level. All that remained was to see to what extent Edward's treachery extended and what the hell was going on over on Hog Island.

Edward did not get up. Wiegard turned and extended his hand to Commissioner Atkinson who had risen from his seat along with Thomas when Wiegard was announced.

"Commissioner, good to see you as always," Wiegard said, shaking the Commissioner's hand with his right hand while patting him on the other arm. It was a politician's handshake and Thomas noticed immediately how much Wiegard smiled. He had a constant smile on his face.

The Commissioner shook Wiegard's hand and then turned to introduce Thomas.

"Mr. Wiegard, this is Mr. Thomas Nash. He is retired British Army and here working on our agricultural production."

Thomas noticed the momentary change in Wiegard's demeanor. A brief expression of surprise crossed the man's face telling him that Wiegard was shocked to see him at Government House.

"A pleasure to meet you," said Wiegard, reaching for Thomas's unoffered hand and shaking it.

"The pleasure is all mine, Herr Wiegard," replied Thomas, using the same salutation that Edward did and hoping that the edge in his voice did not come through.

Wiegard and Thomas remained locked by hand for a few moments staring directly into each other's eyes as if each man was trying to see into the other's thoughts.

"You are too young to be retired from the Army, in these times, because of age, so it must be you suffered some injury eh?" asked Wiegard releasing Thomas's hand and taking a drink from the tray offered by the Butler.

"One might say that," replied Thomas. "But I feel quite fit this evening."

"Yes well we are happy that you are safe and for your service to your country. Now, let's play some cards," Wiegard said, abruptly turning away from Thomas and taking a seat at the card table.

Edward and the Commissioner joined Wiegard at the round table and had chosen their seats. The only one available to Thomas was the one directly opposite Edward. He took his seat and with Wiegard on his right and the Commissioner on his left stared directly at Edward and said.

"Let's see if the superior being can win at cards, your Majesty."

This elicited a chuckle from both Edward and Wiegard and the commissioner reached forward and picked up the deck of cards and began to shuffle them.

After several hands had been dealt the game settled into a predictable pattern. Thomas noticed certain moves made by both the Commissioner and Wiegard that did not make sense to a seasoned poker player and he had the suspicion that both these gentlemen were seasoned players.

They were letting Edward win. The game was a farce. Edward was a farce.

The whole thing was a farce.

Thomas kept playing Edward's words over and over again in his head. This man was aligned one hundred percent with Adolph Hitler. Britain was being bombed on a daily basis by a madman; this man just removed from the throne, supported him. It was unbelievable and his thoughts went back to Churchill and he wondered just how much the old man knew and how much he suspected.

Thomas was paying close attention to the game and he was losing but he was not betting any thing of real value, but now he decided to raise the stakes.

"I say," Thomas started, as he turned in his chair and looked directly at Wiegard. "The best solution I have come up with to expand the pineapple production would be to establish some new farms dedicated to this production. The best place I conclude would be to set it up on Hog Island. It is after all very accessible to Nassau and the port and we would have the room to do it right and really make an impact on the citrus production."

Wiegard stared directly at Thomas and said, with a smile on his face, "Have you been to Hog Island, Mr. Nash?'

"No," Thomas said, knowing that Wiegard knew it was a lie. "But I was hoping to get over there in the next day or so to scout it out."

The exchange had all four of the men's attention and Edward leaned forward in his chair and said, "Hog Island is out of the question. We have some development going on over there and the plans for the island are set. You will just have to find yourself another island to sew your plantation."

"When you say 'We,' Your Highness, are you referring to yourself as the 'Royal We', or are you referring to your Government and administration of this colony?" Thomas asked, turning and facing Edward.

As soon as the words left his mouth he knew that they riled Edward. It was, after all, an insult.

Thomas had noticed that Edward always referred to himself in the plural, as was the custom of the reigning Sovereign. There was just one problem: Edward was not the reigning Sovereign. The reigning Sovereign spoke for Crown and Country and therefore spoke in the plural.

Edward spoke for no one as far as Thomas was concerned.

Not a sound was made and all four men sat in rigid in their positions.

"Mr. Nash," Edward began. "We detect a bit of cheek in your tone and we wish to remind you of your place. Perhaps you are not a man who holds his liquor well."

"I hold my liquor just fine, sir. And as for cheek, I remind your Majesty that if it wasn't for British cheek we would all be goose stepping to Herr Hitler's tune right now."

"And what would be wrong with that!" Wiegard said, slamming his hands down on the table. "It is inevitable that the superior German people are destined to lead the world. Tell me Mr. Nash, are you, like so many of your countrymen blind to the reality, or are you just stupid?"

"Now, now Mr. Wiegard, there is no need for name-calling," Commissioner Atkinson said, interjecting himself for the first time into the conversation.

Thomas leaned forward and waived off the commissioner with his hand, "I will ignore your insult to me and my countrymen because I understand the disease from which you suffer. You believe in the superiority that you deem is held by the German as well as the superiority that comes from your birth but the mistake you make is assuming that the rest of us also believe it. I believe in the superiority of free men and not in the obedience of dogs in the service of a master. I see that Herr Hitler has fooled even the most privileged and educated amongst you but in the end you will be found out and you will be considered the greatest fools of all of history."

"How dare you sir!" shouted Edward rising from the table. "You are the fool because you presume to know things that you have neither the capacity nor the intellect to understand. You will see Mr. Nash, Germany will win this war and we will be returned as the British King. The British don't want me but I am the only one who will save the British race, not Churchill, not that stuttering idiot of a brother of mine and not by diseased scoundrels like you who profess to lecture a King."

"Edward, Edward, Edward," The voice belonged to Wallis and she gently put her hand on Edward's shoulder. "You are too worked up my dear and on such a pleasant evening."

No one had seen Wallis enter the room during the heated exchange amongst Nash, Wiegard and Edward and as she turned from Edward, she faced Thomas.

As heated as he was from his exchange with Edward, Thomas couldn't deny the stirring he instantly felt at the appearance of Wallis.

The men had all risen upon realizing her presence except for Edward who had been standing. He sat down and quickly lit a cigarette.

"Mr. Nash, welcome to Government House I am so sorry I was not here to greet you upon your arrival." said Wallis.

"Thank you Ma'am," Thomas replied.

Wallis then turned her attention to Wiegard and the Commissioner. "Good evening, gentlemen."

"Good evening, ma'am," Wiegard and the Commissioner answered in unison.

"A pity your wife could not join us this evening," Wallis said, addressing the Commissioner directly. "The room is obviously too full of men and so, as is inevitable, the conversation tends to become a little less civilized."

"Quite right, my lady." Wiegard said, casting a glance in Thomas's direction.

He noticed that the salesman's smile was back on Wiegard's face.

"Your presence is sorely needed to add some sense of style and decorum to these rowdy proceedings," Wiegard continued, bowing toward Wallis.

Everyone remained standing except for Edward. Wallis positioned herself next to his chair and then told the men to take their seats. After they had obeyed her command she said. "These poker games are supposed to be an enjoyable and relaxing evening so please do not keep me from spoiling your game, please gentlemen continue. I will just sit here and watch for a little bit."

Thomas had not taken his eyes off of Wallis from the moment he heard her voice. She was a woman in control and her mere presence completely diffused and evened out the situation. He was going to have to keep a lid on things and simmer down.

He had stumbled into a hornet's nest of treachery and he had no doubt that after tipping his hand this evening to Wiegard and Edward that things were going to get a bit dicey.

"I understand ma'am that you are from Baltimore and I have always had a desire to see the Washington, D.C. area," Thomas said, breaking the awkward silence.

"Yes, I am originally from Baltimore but it has been ages since I have been back. I do not have anyone of any consequential value left there so I do not think of it much," replied Wallis.

"Well I am done with this game," said Edward, outing his cigarette in the ashtray in apparent disgust as he stood up.

Wallis stepped aside and Thomas and the others stepped back from the table.

"This evening has been ruined for me. We daresay Nash it is but for the sake of Wallis that we will not cross with you further this evening but you are wrong sir... you and all like minded souls like you, are dead wrong of that we are sure."

And with these words Edward strode out of the room.

So much for British stiff upper lip, Thomas thought to himself. He had definitely gotten under Edward's skin and he liked the feeling of it.

"Your Royal Highness, I do need a moment of your time before you retire for the evening." Wiegard called out, to the departing Edward. "My lady, please excuse me."

"Go ahead run along Rolf you can catch him before he goes upstairs. Have a talk with him and try to calm him down," Wallis said. As Wiegard hurried after Edward she turned to Thomas and smiled. "Whatever did you say to make my husband so distraught?"

Thomas gathered his words for a moment and said, "I apologize Ma'am. I meant no disrespect to you or your household."

He damn well did not have any respect for Edward and he was not going to apologize for disrespecting him.

"We just disagreed, that's all. I will be taking my leave of you now and I thank you for hospitality."

He bowed slightly to Wallis and then turned to Commissioner Atkinson and said,

"Goodnight Commissioner."

"Goodnight, Mr. Nash, I will walk you to the door," replied the Commissioner.

"No need, Commissioner. I can find my own way out."

Thomas turned on his heels and walked out of the large room and toward the front door. As he approached the front of the house the butler met him at the door and offered him an umbrella as it had begun to rain.

He refused the umbrella. The rain would do him good, he thought, cleanse a little of the filth off of him that he felt being in the presence of such treachery.

He stepped out of the opened door and onto the front covered verandah of the house. At the far side of the verandah were four or five steps that led down to the covered portico that was open on both sides. Rolf Wiegard was standing at the end with one foot on the first step, smoking a cigarette.

Thomas adjusted the collar on his jacket and approached Wiegard.

Discarding his cigarette and turning to face Thomas, Wiegard reached out and grasped his right arm. "One word of advice, Mr. Nash. Stay away from Hog Island. Do I make myself clear?"

"Have a good evening, Mr. Wiegard." Thomas replied.

"I am serious," Wiegard said as he tightened his grip of Thomas's forearm over the wound he suffered earlier.

Thomas grimaced instinctively and Wiegard did not notice or believe it was caused by his own strength, but it went ignored.

Thomas wrestled his hand away from Wiegard and moved past him and onto the first step and with his back to him, he said,

"I suggest you go inside and seek shelter from this rain, Herr Wiegard. There are things out here right now that could harm you."

Thomas walked down the steps to the street below as the rain began to come down harder.

<hr />

Wiegard entered the Governor's mansion after his confrontation with Nash in a foul mood. This new player was obviously provocative and he wasn't exactly thrilled with the latest development. He was also angry with himself for losing his temper. He had fed off of Edward's hostility and he knew better. Damn Edward, he thought. How was the man going to win the British people over for Hitler if he couldn't handle one obstinate Englishman like Nash?

He found Edward sitting on the verandah that ran along the outside of his dressing room, smoking a cigarette. "Has your wife gone to bed sir?" Wiegard asked as he sat down in a chair opposite Edward.

"Perhaps you would like to join her?" Edward answered, turning and looking directly at Wiegard.

Wiegard was momentarily shocked by Edward's biting tone but recovered his control and decided to ignore Edward's question. It was obvious the man knew about his and Wallis's trysts and it was obvious he was still upset from the earlier encounter with Nash.

"This Nash character is a nobody, your Grace," Wiegard began. "You shouldn't have lost your temper and allowed him to provoke you like that."

"Provoke me?" Edward replied. "The man was the picture of insolence and we will not stand for it."

"You're going to face a lot worse when you re-ascend the throne," Wiegard said, taking a seat next to Edward. "You are sadly mistaken if you think all of Britain will just lay down and accept Hitler as their master. You are the chosen one, precisely because you are the only one the Furher sees as having the ability to win the peace between the people of Britain and Germany. I remind you sir," he paused, "Your royal subjects will need your strength to guide them."

Turning to face Wiegard, Edward pulled an envelope out of his jacket pocket. "We received this letter this morning from our brother the King, informing us that our nieces Elizabeth and Margaret will be unable to join us this Christmas after all. Apparently they refuse to leave their parents side while London is being bombed."

Wiegard was secretly relieved, one less complication to worry about, but he could tell that Edward was upset about the King's decision. 'That's a pity," he began. "I know that you and Wallis were so looking forward to their visit, does she know?"

"No she does not, we have made all sorts of preparations," Edward said, folding the letter and returning it to his jacket pocket. "Magnanimity is not our best suit but we will wear it and wear it well until the time comes for us to be less than magnanimous with our brother and that wife of his."

Rising from his chair, Wiegard walked to the north side of the verandah and stared in the direction of Hog Island. "You will go down in history as the King who won the peace," he said, without turning and facing Edward directly. "You are the only one who sees that uniting the two great Aryan peoples, the Germans and the British is the only way to defeat the communists before they can wreck the world," turning and facing Edward directly, he continued. "History will treat you better than your brother has," and bowing ever so slightly, added, "your Majesty."

CHAPTER TWENTY-SEVEN

Saturday, November 8ᵗʰ, 1941
6:00 a.m.
Hanson Family Motor Yacht
Miami, Florida

Oliver Blackwood stood on the deck of Jonathan Hanson's 52-foot motor launch admiring how father and daughter worked in unison to prepare the craft for departure. The crew had been given a week's worth of wages and told to take a few days off to enjoy the sights and scenes of Miami. This voyage would have only three passengers: Blackwood, Jonathan Hanson and his daughter Nancy – both accomplished sailors. Blackwood was confident the short voyage would be without incident.

As he watched Nancy run through the checklist for setting sail, his mind wondered back to the first time he had met her when she was only six years old. He would arrive, from time to time, at her father's home and the little girl would screech with delight and fly into his arms upon seeing him. He remembered with fondness her putting her foot down when her father tried to send her to bed one late evening. Nancy then informed her father that Uncle Oliver was the most exciting person in the world, and since she could not sleep, and since she hated her dolls, she would much rather stay up and visit with Uncle Oliver.

Over dinner and drinks the previous evening, the two men had laid it all out to her. She showed no signs of surprise, as Blackwood expected, and she had agreed to her role without any hesitation. She was, after all, Jonathan Hanson's daughter and Blackwood had no doubt as to her mental toughness.

She told both men of her and the Commissioner's suspicion of Wiegard, but she expressed amazement at Edward and Wallis's treachery. Her father explained it all quite thoroughly when he told her that chaos always presented an opportunity to make a vast fortune and although his primary motivation was patriotic, he was going to make a fortune off of what was happening in Nassau and Hog Island. She was his one and only heir; she needed to understand how the game was played.

Her mission was quite simple, get Oliver Blackwood and her father quietly and discreetly into Nassau, keep the boat ready and follow Oliver Blackwood's lead.

The sun was just rising over the Biscayne Bay when he heard Nancy come up from behind him and say in a soft voice, "Everything will be fine uncle Oliver."

"Of course it will, my dear," he responded. "I hope you're all right with everything."

"Yes, of course Uncle Oliver." Replied Nancy turning toward the old man and smiling. "Have you had your tea yet this morning?"

"No, not yet," Oliver Blackwood replied. "I don't profess to knowing my way around a ship's galley."

"Come on, then," Nancy said, taking Oliver Blackwood by the hand and leading him back into the cabin. "I do know my way around the galley and I am going to fix us both a cup of tea."

━╬ ╬━

Saturday, November 8th, 1941
6:30 a.m.
Royal Victoria Hotel
Nassau, Bahamas

Thomas reached for his watch knocking over the empty whiskey bottle on the nightstand. He sat up and started to rub his right eye. It took him a moment to focus but as best he could tell it was about 6:30 in the morning.

He had hardly slept: the empty whiskey bottle and the smashed radio that he had taken off of his captor were a testament to how he had dealt with the preceding evening's festivities. He had controlled his rage to a point and upon returning to his room at the Royal Victoria Hotel, he destroyed the radio.

He had not planned on destroying the radio, but when he entered his room he saw it lying out on top of a chest of drawers and his anger boiled over – with one quick motion, he threw it against the wall and smashed it to bits. Thomas Nash then sat down facing the door; Gun in one hand, whiskey bottle in the other.

In the hours that passed, he never cooled down. His encounter with Edward and Wiegard had left him in a permanent mood of rage. As the dawn was breaking, his decision was made.

He was going to kill Edward, but that wouldn't be enough. Before that, he was going to destroy the caves and the chemicals on Hog Island and *then* he would kill Edward after making sure the bastard understood that his plans had been destroyed.

He got up and walked over to the bathroom. He needed to get cleaned up, he was hungry and he needed to find Franklyn.

They were going back to Hog Island tonight but he needed to get a hold of some things first and the boy was proving to be very resourceful.

He looked at himself in the mirror. He looked like hell, he thought to himself. Maybe that was what he was supposed to look like, someone who was in hell, after all, he thought, that's where he would be headed for killing a King even one as traitorous as Edward.

The thought was broken by three strong knocks on his hotel door.

"Who is it?" he called out, cocking his gun and bracing for whatever was on the other side.

"Commissioner Atkinson, may I have a moment of your time?"

Thomas hesitated only a moment and then opened the door allowing Commissioner Atkinson to enter the room.

Closing the door behind him he addressed the Commissioner. "Wee bit early in the morning for socializing, wouldn't you say sir?"

The Commissioner smiled. "I know who you are, Mr. Nash, and I know why you are here. I pray for your soul sir and for mine as I have been ordered to assist you in any way I can."

Despite the empty liquor bottle and the commissioner's somber words, Thomas's instincts kicked in. *Did Oliver Blackwood's reach touch the Commissioner? Who had ordered him to assist, and was this all a trap?*

"Do you know exactly what has been going on over at Hog Island?" he asked, indicating a chair for the commissioner to take a seat.

Commissioner Atkinson remained standing.

"I have my suspicions and I know that Wiegard is a Nazi zealot, so I cannot imagine it being anything good."

Thomas's mouth twitched as he lit a cigarette, snapping the lighter shut, he spat out,

"They are building a weapon a missile and there are chemicals involved. This little backwater island that you are supposed to police is the center of some grand chemical experiment and that Nazi-loving bastard Wiegard is nothing compared to the traitor that His Royal Highness Edward Duke of Windsor, Governor General of the Bahamas and disgraced weak-souled abdicator is."

'I know," the commissioner replied, in such a subdued and melancholy tone that it's sadness took Thomas by surprise.

"It has been very difficult for me to come to terms with the depth of Edward's treachery. I have admired him for a long time and it has caused me great dread to realize that he is a traitor to his country." The Commissioner paused and then looked directly at Thomas, "A traitor King...who would have thought it?"

Thomas recognized the emotion as he himself had wondered as to the reality of Edward actually being a traitor but the doubt no longer existed and he had come to terms with what he was going to do.

The Commissioner, as though reading Thomas's mind, rose from his seat and opened the door to leave. With his back to Thomas he said, "Cocktails are always at 8 p.m. at Government house. We will all be gathered there this evening."

With those words, Commissioner Atkinson walked out of Thomas's hotel room closing the door behind him.

⊷ ⊶

Saturday, November 8th, 1941
7 a.m.
Wiegard Residence
Nassau, Bahamas

Krueger had not slept the entire night. He was haunted by Nash's escape from Hog Island and he had been stationed outside Government House when the exchange between Wiegard and Nash occurred.

The incident that had distracted him from his interrogation of Nash, back in the caves, was actually a breakthrough. The guard who had alerted him mistook the scientist's jubilation as another accident.

Wiegard had been furious with him for losing Nash and had ordered him to stay outside at Government House while he went in to the poker game.

After the confrontation with Wiegard and Nash was over, Krueger had followed Nash to the Royal Victoria Hotel and camped outside until 4 a.m. Convinced Nash was not going anywhere, he reluctantly returned to Wiegard's residence before the sun came up.

Wiegard was waiting for him when he arrived at the house, and informed him that the time had come to shut down the Hog Island operation. He issued orders to Krueger to instruct the scientists to pack up everything and prepare to board a ship that would return them to Germany.

Kruger boarded the launch and headed out to Hog Island to carry out the orders. The trip allowed him time to think and he decided at that moment that he was going to have to take a risk.

He knew Nash was no farmer; he had his sore body to remind him of the man's skills. No, this man was military and this man was on a mission.

The question was just what mission was Nash on. Were they on the same mission? He knew that approaching Nash directly was not the way to go but he also knew that Nash would return to Hog Island.

That would be the place to confront him.

This time, Krueger would be ready. This time, he would have the element of surprise. He knew in his gut that things were coming to a head and as he approached Hog Island, he said a little prayer asking the almighty to guide his judgment.

CHAPTER TWENTY-EIGHT

June 6ᵗʰ, 2013
Katherine Blackwood's garage

Katherine led Nicholas out through the back door of the kitchen and to a large detached shed at the back of her property. The moon provided enough light to mark the cobblestone pathway that led from the kitchen door.

The night summer air had a slight sense of dampness to it and Nicholas filled his lungs with deep breaths almost as if trying to refuel his mind. A soft yellow light emerged from the shed as Katherine unhitched the door and opened it, revealing Andrew Stone's red Triumph Spitfire.

Katherine stepped aside, allowing Nicholas to enter before her. He slowly walked up to the car and a rush of emotions flowed over him. The car was stunning. The black top was folded down and buttoned up neatly to the back of the car bonnet. The red was a deep almost crimson and in the soft yellow light of the shed, the car glowed.

"It's beautiful," Nicholas said, passing his hand over the front fender and moving it up to the windshield. "The lines are so simple yet so elegant," He continued, as he walked toward the back of the car.

He looked into the car's interior and touched the caramel leather seat with the tips of his fingers. He noticed that the shift knob was a little worn, and the realization occurred to him that his father's hand had worn that shift knob down.

"Go on," she said, smiling at Nicholas. "Get in, feel around a bit."

"I'm a little bit overwhelmed to be honest."

Katherine's smile gave him a bit of a reprieve. "I understand," she said. "It's been a busy evening and I've put a lot on you tonight."

She came up next to Nicholas and also placed her hand on the Spitfire. "This was your father's favorite place. He would come out here in the evenings and sit at that old desk over there," she said, indicating a small wooden desk and chair in the corner of the garage. "And read his paper. He would spend hours polishing the car with a soft cloth. This old garage was his sanctuary, his spot of peace in his very irrational world."

Nicholas scanned the entire garage and in his mind's eye, envisioned his father sitting at the desk puffing on a pipe and reading the Sunday Times. "I can't thank you enough for bringing me out here," he said, turning to face Katherine. "I can almost feel him and I never thought that I would ever feel him again. I'm overcome, I really am."

They both stood there for a long time, each lost in their thoughts before Katherine broke the silence.

"I am ill. And part of me wishes that I had done what I am doing now a long time ago."

She smiled as Nicholas turned to face her. "I have an inoperable form of cancer and it will get the better of me. My intent this evening was to tell you about the unsung heroes of 1941 and the story of your father with the desire that you would respect and keep the memory and service of these great men alive after I am gone. I cannot tell you how to proceed or how to accomplish that and from where I will be it really will not matter much, but it is my hope that you will take these secrets and these sins, treat them and these great men with the dignity and the respect they deserve and ensure that their actions are presented in a manner that honors their service and sacrifices. They, after all, did the difficult things that saved the world... They at least deserve that."

Nicholas found himself fighting back tears. Thirty-six hours earlier he had never heard of Katherine Blackwood and now, he felt an overwhelming sense of sadness at the idea of losing her.

After a long moment, he spoke in a whisper.

"I am very sorry to hear you are so ill. I don't really know what to say."

Katherine smiled.

"There isn't anything much to say and I do not want you feeling bad or sorry for me. I have had a wonderful life and my only regret is that I did not meet you until it was too late, but enough of that. This story is far from over ... things do come to a head and the darkest secret is yet to be revealed. The night of November 8th, 1941, it would all come undone."

"We are going to need some more tea."

CHAPTER TWENTY-NINE

Saturday, November 8th, 1941
7 p.m.
Jonathan Hanson's yacht
Nassau, Bahamas

The voyage from Miami had been uneventful and a few minutes past seven in the evening, Oliver Blackwood stood next to Nancy Atkinson, marveling at how effortlessly she maneuvered the craft into a mooring at the docks in front of the straw market. The vendors had long packed up and headed home for the evening so there were very few people around. No one paid any attention to the yacht as she docked.

Jonathan Hanson scrambled ashore like a man half his age and secured the yacht's lines while Nancy cut the engines and then proceeded to set the back lines.

Blackwood had spent the majority of the trip below deck reading a book. He knew that Hanson wanted the time to speak privately with Nancy. Father and daughter had stayed above deck for most of the trip engaged in deep conversation.

Oliver Blackwood still didn't believe that his friend was being upfront with him and suspected that Jonathan Hanson had an additional motive for being on this trip.

"All secure," Hanson announced, as both he and Nancy joined Oliver Blackwood in the main salon.

"Right, I am off to find David and head up to Government House," Nancy said, stringing her small purse across her shoulder.

"Give me an hour, Daddy and then meet us at Government House. Cocktails are always at 8, and do not fret Uncle Oliver," she said turning to face him. "All is in hand. Things will all work out exactly as you planned, have no doubt."

"I never do," Blackwood responded, taking Nancy's hands in his. "Since you were six years old I have known how strong and capable you are." With that he planted a small kiss on her forehead. Nancy climbed ashore and headed up to her residence on Parliament Street to catch her husband.

Jonathan Hanson and Oliver Blackwood watched as she walked away.

"All right, old boy," Hanson said. "We have an hour to kill before we have to head out. Let's have a drink or two and discuss exactly how you want to cut up the company, and exactly how we are going to have to hide everything from Congress and the God damn Justice Department."

Oliver Blackwood smiled and followed his friend into the main salon. Typical Jonathan, he thought. Always working, always worrying about the next problem.

He, on the other hand, was still worried about tonight.

⊷⊶

Saturday, November 8th, 1941
7:00 p.m.
Hog Island

Krueger had been on Hog Island all day going through the cave complex and the area around the caves with precision. The scientists and the guards had broken everything down as Wiegard had ordered. Krueger could sense the excitement, amongst the usually dour scientists, at the prospect of their return home.

The crew worked with a sense of urgency. After all, they had been isolated for so long that the thought of returning to their homeland and civilization was overwhelming.

Krueger was a little surprised at how quickly the work had wound up but there was no doubt about it, two fully armed and operational missiles sat ready for transport just inside the mouth of the cave.

It was now just past 7:30 in the evening and he had positioned himself behind the tree line that ran along the first ridge up from the beach cove, where he figured Nash had come ashore the previous time.

He had taken up the position as soon as darkness had fallen. Krueger had thought nonstop since the previous evening about exactly how he was going to handle the confrontation that was coming.

He had a sense that he and this Nash fellow had more in common than appeared but he had not forgotten the last time they had met, his ribs still sore, a reminder that this man was no slouch. He was a professional, and this gave Krueger hope that maybe they could work together. Nash was either going to help him or he was going to have to kill him. Either way, the moment was fast approaching.

He checked his entire site lines, took a sip of water from a canteen in his pocket and settled in for the wait.

Saturday, November 8th, 1941
7:30 p.m.
Hog Island

Thomas admired Franklyn's skill with the small craft as he guided the sloop toward the same cut on the south side of Hog Island that they had landed on two nights before. The boy had exceeded his expectations in rounding up the supplies Thomas had requested but coming up with dynamite, was too good to be true.

Franklyn had made several trips to load the boat with extra gasoline the and then on his last trip to a construction site to look for additional gas containers, he found six sticks of dynamite.

The dynamite was used to blast away the limestone and for clearing out rocky formations. Franklyn had found one of the sheds unlocked and all the workers on the other side of the site. He entered the shack, pilfered around, found the dynamite, and took off running all the way back to the boat where he breathlessly confessed to Thomas his crime.

＝‖＝

Krueger spotted the small boat as she slid thru the cut in the island and worked her way up to the beach. He felt his pulse quicken and he did an automatic check of his weapon without taking his eyes off of the craft.

A young black boy guided the boat with the gentle sculling of an oar right up the sandy beach and Nash jumped out and grabbed the front of the boat to steady her while the boy stowed away the oar and jumped onto the beach next to him.

"Right, secure the line to that tree up there and then let's load up and head for those caves," Nash said, tossing the rope to the boy, who scurried twenty yards up the beach and looped the rope around a coconut tree.

Thomas reached into the boat and pulled out a large canvas bag and four large plastic containers of gasoline.

"All secure, Boss" the boy whispered, as he sidled up next to Thomas and started to load one of the canvas sacks onto his back.

"I'll carry both bags, lad, just help me strap them on. That way, I'll be able to carry two of the gasoline containers and you can carry the other two."

The boy nodded and proceeded to help Thomas strap on the canvas bags that contained the dynamite sticks and some other items stuffed into a smaller sack.

With the bags secured on his back, Thomas picked up a gasoline container in each hand and turned toward the tree line and the path to the caves.

As he turned around, he came face to face with Krueger, who now had a handgun pointed directly at his chest.

Thomas froze and locked eyes with Krueger.

"Get down from there, boy," Krueger called to Franklyn.

Franklyn turned his head and immediately saw the gun, slowly dropping what he was doing; he climbed down from the boat and onto the sand to face Krueger.

"Good boy," Krueger said, pointing with his left index finger toward the ground indicated to Franklyn that he was to lay face down in the sand.

Once Franklyn was down on the ground, Krueger turned his attention to Thomas. He had never taken his eyes off of him and the gun had not moved an inch and was still pointed at the man's heart. Thomas had not moved a muscle and he continued to hold the two gasoline containers in his hands, a feat of strength that was not lost on Krueger.

"You may put those gasoline containers down if you wish."

Thomas waited a moment, relaxed his grip and placed the containers down next to his feet.

"I have been trying to figure out exactly who you are, Mr. Nash."

"Is that a question?" Thomas said.

"No," replied Krueger, stealing a quick glance in Franklyn's direction. "I pretty much figured it out. You fight like a soldier; you're running around loose in places you have no business being in, unless of course it is your business to be snooping around restricted places.

Only a madman on a mission would be doing whatever it is you are attempting to do here tonight."

There was no reply from Thomas and Krueger half-expected such. "Well, which is it Mr. Nash?"

"Which is what?"

"Are you crazy or are you on a mission? And if you are on a mission, it just might be possible that we are on the same one."

"Unless I am mistaken," Thomas began. "You are the man in charge of Mr. Wiegard's little laboratory project, so I sincerely doubt that we are on the same mission."

"Ah, but looks may be deceiving, Mr. Nash. Perhaps you might consider alternative possibilities. Let me explain things as I see them.

"First, you are standing on a beach on Hog Island with containers of gasoline and God knows what in that backpack of yours."

"Dynamite" Thomas said.

"Dynamite, very nice. Well, that will do the trick if your intent is to blow up the caves." There was a long pause and Krueger continued in a softer voice. "If that is your intent, then we very well may be on the same mission."

⟞⟊⟊⟞

Thomas heard Krueger, but his instinct told him it was all a ruse. There was no chance they were on the same side. This man, after all, was in charge here on Hog Island and as such, was part of the whole damn treachery.

"I don't think we are on the same team." Thomas said, not taking his eyes off of Krueger's pistol.

"I can understand your skepticism but perhaps I can change your mind. Do you have the radio you took off of me last night?" Krueger said, lowering the gun for the first time. He still held the weapon by his side but Thomas sensed the gesture was designed to diffuse the tension a bit.

"I do."

"Get it out."

Thomas slowly slipped off the smaller backpack and with one eye on Krueger opened it up and removed the radio from inside. He tossed it to the sand in front of Krueger's feet.

Without looking down, Krueger said, "What the hell happened to my radio?"

"A momentary lapse of reason," Thomas answered.

"Well if you examined it, and I am sure you did, you realized that it's U.S. Army issued and not the typical radio communication device one buys in a store."

Thomas had already come to that conclusion.

Krueger continued. "That radio was my method of contact with the American Navy and my purpose is to steal the missiles and the technology being developed here, get them into the hands of the U.S. Navy and stop

Wiegard from ever delivering them to the German Navy for use."

"Now," he said raising the gun once more and pointing it at Thomas. "What is your mission here, Mr. Nash? I am running out of patience."

Thomas digested what Krueger had just told him but he did not let his guard down.

"Just because you have an American Army radio does not mean a damn thing. You work for Wiegard and if what you are saying is true, you have had ample time and opportunity to destroy this mess. You don't need me to do it."

"Good point. But you are here, aren't you? I needed to wait until the missiles were complete. Now I have a decision to make.

"Do I trust you or do I kill you? And if I kill you, then I have to kill your young friend laying there in the sand."

Out of the corner of his eye, Thomas saw Franklyn flinch.

The two men continued to stare at each other with Krueger holding the gun straight out and pointed directly at Thomas.

The moment seemed to last forever and then Krueger quickly spun the gun around in his hand so as the handle was now facing away from himself and handed it to Thomas startling him in the process.

"You now have the gun, Mr. Nash. I either just made the biggest mistake of my life or you are the man I think you are and this will prove that we are on the same team."

It was an extraordinary move on Krueger's part and Thomas was initially stunned by the action but he recovered quickly and took control of the gun. Krueger had just laid it all out on the line and he had just committed himself to a very brave course of action.

Thomas made the decision right then and there that he was going to throw in with this man Krueger and see where it all went.

Lowering the gun, he said,

"I have six sticks of dynamite and some gasoline. I want to blow those damn caves to bits."

Krueger smiled. "Well, let's get started; we've wasted enough time with these formalities. We can get to the caves in about twenty minutes if we move quickly. Leave the gasoline, there's a huge supply in the cave itself; bring the dynamite. That will be a nice touch. Let's move."

With those words, Krueger turned and started walking up toward the tree line.

"Up and at 'em lad," Thomas called out to Franklyn. "You're not going to die quite yet."

Franklyn scrambled up from the sand and dusted himself off. Thomas had already fallen in behind Krueger and Franklyn followed suit.

CHAPTER THIRTY

Saturday November 8th, 1941 - 8:30 PM.
Government House - Nassau

Rolf Wiegard sipped his drink half-heartedly listening to Wallis as she rambled on about some minor irritation. He looked up when the butler announced the arrival of Commissioner and Nancy Atkinson. He found himself relieved to have someone other than Wallis and Edward to talk to.

Edward turned and welcomed their arrival. "Good evening, Commissioner, and my dear Nancy, so happy to have you back on our little island."

"It is so good to be home," Nancy replied, squeezing the commissioner's hand. "How are you, your Majesty? You seem happy this evening."

"We are more than happy my dear. We are, shall we say, fulfilled. Come, say hello to Wallis she is of course bereft of friends when you are off the island."

Nancy and Wallis exchanged a light kiss and it was then that Wiegard noticed the change in the commissioner's demeanor. He had refused his customary gin and tonic and instead had instructed the butler to bring him a glass of water.

This change bothered Wiegard. Now that the hour was near, his senses were on high alert for anything out of the ordinary. The Commissioner's manner did not sit well with him. People were creatures of habit and when they broke those habits, it was an indication that something was out of order.

Earlier in the evening, he had delivered fantastic and exciting news to Edward and Wallis. The work on Hog Island was complete. In three weeks' time the United States Government and its military would lie in ruins, Britain would be forced to sue for peace, the war would be over, and Edward would once again ascend to the throne.

Wiegard's meticulous engineering had made it all possible and now that finely disciplined and tuned engineer's ability warned him that something was off with the Commissioner.

The man was on to something and this made Wiegard a little nervous. He looked at his watch and thought about Krueger. He had told him that he wanted to go out to Hog Island and just make sure that everything was in order and that was around three o' clock. The hour was approaching nine and Krueger had yet to check in with him.

The scientist and the guards who had made the caves of Hog Island their home and workplace had been busy dismantling and packing up all of the equipment that was going to be shipped back to Germany on the same ship that was going to return them to the fatherland, their families and the adoring embrace of Adolph Hitler and the German people.

Wiegard had told them all a great tale of how upon their arrival in Germany they would be accorded the highest of honors and that their names would go down in history as men who served the Reich and the Fuhrer and whose isolated dedication produced the instrument that brought a terrible and horrible war to a just and fitting end. Only he knew the truth. The cargo ship that would leave Hog Island with the scientists, guards and equipment all packed on board would never been seen from or heard from again. Of this, Wiegard was certain.

The group settled into polite conversation with Wallis asking Nancy all sorts of questions about her trip to the U.S. and her visit with her family. This time, however, Wallis refrained from her usual complaining and griping about this miserable little island, as she liked to refer to Nassau.

Commissioner Atkinson for the most part had not uttered more than a few phrases and then he cleared his throat and said, "I must say, your Royal Highnesses are in such good spirits this evening. Is there any good news that the rest of us are unaware of? Because from where I sit, this war is going very badly for Britain and I see little reason to be so damn spirited."

The words were delivered in a low but resonating growl and everyone, including Nancy, was taken aback by the Commissioner's bluntness and tone.

"Why so serious, David?" Wallis said, with a slight laugh in her voice. "It is a lovely evening and we are amongst friends, no reason to be so gloomy, that horrible war is far from these shores and we must just wait things out until they get better."

Wallis voice helped soothe the moment but the Commissioner was not quite finished and with as much charm as he could muster given his present display, he said.

"Forgive me madam for not sharing your optimism. I see things going very poorly for my country and I do not expect you, as an American, to understand that."

This was the second stunning thing the Commissioner had said since he arrived.

Nancy Atkinson sensing her husband's anger was getting the better of him spoke up. "Now, now, David. There is no reason to be insulting; no one here is insensitive to Britain's predicament and, after all, you yourself are married to an American. Or have I been away so long that you have forgotten?"

Her words carried enough levity in them to cut the tension and the Commissioner turned and addressed Wallis directly.

"Please forgive my boorish and rude behavior. My wife, as always, is correct and I apologize for offending you. Perhaps I am just getting a little grumpy in my old age."

"We all get a little grumpy sometimes, my good man. Come on, have another drink," Edward said, slapping the Commissioner on the back. "This war will soon be over and then we can all go home."

Wiegard cringed at Edward's comment. It was true the war was going poorly for Britain but even he was amazed at the craven callousness of Edward's remarks. My God, he thought, does the man not have one humble bone in his body? The Commissioner was an Englishman and a veteran. He decided to change the subject and addressed Nancy.

"My dear, how did you get such lovely colour to your cheeks?"

Nancy smiled at Wiegard's offensive charm. "How very clever of you Rolf, to combine the colour of my cheeks in such a manner as to be a little cheeky yourself." Laughing, she squeezed his arm, "My cheeks have this ruddy red colour to them because I motored over from Miami this morning along with my father and we spent the whole day bathed in the sun and wind."

"Your father is here in Nassau?" Wiegard asked.

"Yes, he is aboard his yacht, she is docked in the harbour right now, I hope you do not mind your Highness," Nancy said, turning to Edward. "But I told him to come up the hill to Government House and have a drink with us."

"Mind, mind, of course not!" Edward almost jumped up from his seat. "We are very happy to have his company. We wish he had known of his pending arrival; we most certainly would have arranged something a little nicer for such a distinguished gentleman."

"You are too kind, your Majesty. My father speaks very fondly of you and he always mentions how much he enjoys visiting with you and Wallis when he is in Nassau – that is why I knew you would not object to my inviting him up."

Edward clasped his hands together and looked at Wallis.

"What a fine evening this is turning out to be. We must remember it my dear remind me to make note of it in our diary. First Nancy returns and now we hear that her father is joining us as well, let's get word to the kitchen that we are having a party."

Wallis laughed and said, "I will ring the butler and tell him to get everyone up and busy one more for dinner."

"Actually two more," interjected Nancy.

"Two more?" asked Edward.

"Yes, my father has brought along an old friend; you may know him. Oliver Blackwood."

Wiegard watched the colour drain from Edward's face at the mention of Oliver Blackwood's name.

CHAPTER THIRTY-ONE

Saturday, November 8th, 1941
8:15 p.m.
Hog Island

It had taken Thomas, Franklyn, and Krueger less than twenty minutes to hike the distance from the beach to the entrance of the caves. Thomas had acknowledged to Krueger that he was sent by London to poke around but he chose not to reveal the bits about Edward and Wallis; he would deal with them after this little business on Hog Island was complete and he and Krueger parted ways.

Krueger seemed convincing enough that he was just an American who worked security for Wiegard but was not about to allow his country to be a target for the weapons being developed on Hog Island. The radio, Krueger explained, was his way of contacting the U.S. military for assistance in stealing the weapons.

Krueger had a plan all worked out. He was going to tell the guards the truth about their destiny and then he was going to load them all on board one of Wiegard's large personal boats and point them toward Florida. Then he was going to secure the missiles and seal the caves.

Thomas had not even given the guards or scientists a second thought and as far as he was concerned they were all nothing but a bunch of lousy Nazis. He would just as soon kill them than save them.

They came upon the ridge that overlooked the entrance to the caves. Two of the guards and a scientist were smoking out in front of the cave entrance when Krueger, Thomas and Franklyn walked down the ridge. As they approached, Krueger called out to one of the guards. Ansell.

"Ansell, get everybody out of the caves and get them now. I need to talk to everyone."

Ansell hesitated, wondering about the appearance of Thomas and Franklyn along with Krueger and did not respond immediately, which was too long a time for Krueger.

"Ansell!" Krueger snapped. "I said I want everybody out of the cave and gathered here in front of me and I want it done now."

The young American's tone had the effect of snapping Ansell out of his thoughts and trance and he immediately spun on his toes and ran into the caves to round up the others.

Good obedient Nazi dog, Thomas thought. Just yell at these bastards and they will snap to attention.

The scientists and guards gathered in front of the cave and Krueger addressed them.

"There will be no ship to take you home."

The statement was made matter of fact and only met by a shuffling of feat by those gathered.

"There is only one way off of this island for you, and you're all going to have to leave now and you are going to have to do exactly as I tell you."

"But we do not understand, Herr Krueger," Karl, the lead scientist, said. "Herr Wiegard just told us this morning that we would be returning home on board a freighter and that we would be received as heroes. Now you are saying what? We cannot go home? I do not understand."

There was genuine distress in Karl's voice but Krueger was quick to respond.

"Karl, I am only going to repeat myself one more time. If you stay here you will die, if you leave on any freighter Wiegard puts you on, you will die. Your only chance of survival is to do exactly as I say."

The collection of guards and scientists were more unsettled. Muted conversation broke out amongst the group.

Thomas stood back and almost grudgingly admired their stiff resolve in the face of what they were being told. He had to admit that these men had been disciplined enough to work in isolation on Hog Island and there was something to their strength of character to respect.

"Quiet!" said Karl to the scientist and guards, and then turning to Krueger. "I do not know why I believe you, but I do. What is your plan to save us, Herr Krueger?"

Krueger adopted a softer tone now that the news had been delivered.

"I want all of you to get on board the large launch we have docked in the l harbor here. The boat is large enough to safely transport you and I want you to follow the compass and head 295 degrees towards Miami. The weather is fine, the sea is flat and you will be in Miami in eight hours."

"Miami ... America. How can we go to America? What do we say when we arrive?" Karl had assumed the spokesperson role for the group.

"I have a radio here," Krueger said showing the tip of the damaged radio. "This radio is used to contact the American authorities. I will alert them that you are coming and that you are to be taken care of."

"Why would the Americans take care of us?"

"Because I am going to tell them to take care of you."

"Forgive me, Herr Krueger, but we did not know you were so powerful to command the Americans."

"Karl, I appreciate your concerns but you are going to have to trust me. There is no problem with you and the Americans. Remember, America is neutral in this war and I will see to it that you are taken care of. The alternative is to stay here and die."

The effect of the words took a few moments to settle in. Karl then turned to the other Germans assembled and spoke to them. After a few minutes, he spoke.

"We are ready to trust you and go to Miami."

"Good. You have five minutes to gather whatever personal belongings you want and then meet me down at the dock."

The Germans dispersed into the caves and in a matter of minutes they had reassembled in front of the entrance.

Krueger turned to Thomas and Franklyn. "I am going to take these guys down to the launch and get them set to go," he said. "You two go into the cave and get the two completed missiles moved to the front and retrieve the three large containers of gas that are stored in the back."

Thomas had not said a word, but had found himself impressed by Krueger's command of the situation and he jokingly clicked his heals together and said,

"Yavolt mein commandant."

Before waiting for a reaction from Krueger, Thomas turned to Franklyn "Heads up lad, let's get a move on."

Krueger and the Germans headed to the launch and Thomas and Franklyn entered the caves.

It did not take long for Thomas and Franklyn to locate the gas containers that Krueger had mentioned and they dragged them to the front of the caves. The two missiles were completed and already loaded on a trolley that made them easy to transport to the front of the cave entrance. Thomas could not help but be impressed by the missiles themselves. The missile casings were painted a battleship black and both had fins on the back, which he assumed had something to do with the aerodynamics and pointed tips that were painted a different shade of black – not necessarily readily apparent.

As Thomas and Franklyn finished rolling the missiles to the front of the cave, Krueger came up from the dock.

"They're off. If they don't screw it up, they should make Miami by morning."

"Was that all hogwash about contacting the Americans to help them, or were you serious?" Thomas asked.

"I am serious. I can contact the U.S. Navy and they will escort them in, but I also need to call the Navy to pick up these missiles."

What the hell are their effectiveness?" asked Thomas, as he ran his hand along one of the missiles.

"I would be careful if I were you," Krueger said. "You can't use one of these missiles to blow up the caves."

Thomas smiled; Krueger was very adroit at reading people.

"Well let's get on with it then. What do you suggest?"

"Here is my plan. Get that dynamite out that you brought along. I want to seal these damn caves; there are still chemical inside and then I want to get these missiles on board the second launch I have here. I want to get them into Nassau and wait for the U.S. Navy to arrange to pick them up."

"Well, I tell you what. You and Franklyn here get the missiles on board," Thomas said. "I will set the dynamite and then we'll blow the hell out of this place and head back to Nassau, I have one more piece of business to take care of this evening and then it will be time to go home."

With those words, the three of them sprang into action. Krueger and Franklyn rolled the missile cart through the sand and down to the dock that housed the second launch.

Thomas entered the cave and examined the equipment the German scientists had left packed and stacked ready for shipping. The crates were made of wood and stenciled with some German words that he did not understand but it didn't matter. He was going to blow the place sky-high and then he was going to deal with his Majesty. Thomas could feel the adrenalin in him begin to build and he realized that he was going to enjoy killing Edward.

It took about fifteen minutes for him to wire up the dynamite and run a fuse out into the clearing in front of the caves. He had strategically placed the containers of gasoline so as the explosion would cause a fire and burn the entire inside of the caves including the leftover equipment. If he had done his job correctly, the explosion would cause the walls of the cave to collapse and seal the entrance.

Krueger and Franklyn came up from the boat dock and Franklyn spoke.

"All is ready boss, let's get the hell outta here I gots a bad feeling it's time for us to go."

"Just a few more minutes son and we will be on our way. "

Thomas double-checked the fuse line and then turned to Krueger.

"Would you like to do the honors?" He said holding out his butane lighter to Krueger.

"I think you have come from a bit farther away from me for this moment, so I will let you strike the match. I agree with your man Franklyn here, let's get the hell out of here."

Thomas turned and snapped open the top of the lighter. With a final look around he lit the end of the fuse and watched it catch fire.

"Right, let's get a move on. This fuse will burn down in three minutes and I want to be off this damn rock when it blows."

Franklyn did not hesitate. He had seen what one stick of dynamite could do on the construction site and he knew that Thomas had used all six of the sticks they had brought along and the gas and dynamite connection. This boom was going to be a big one.

The three men scrambled aboard the launch and Franklyn loosened the mooring lines while Krueger fired up the engine and guided the craft out of its berth and away from Hog Island. All three men kept looking back toward Hog Island. More than four minutes passed and Thomas was beginning to think that he had done something wrong when the explosion hit.

The noise was deafening and then the fire shot up into a giant plume lighting the surrounding trees on fire. The effect of the burning trees lit the whole island in an eerie glow.

Krueger turned his attention to the task at hand and headed the launch in the direction of Nassau Harbour.

CHAPTER THIRTY-TWO

Saturday, November 7th, 1941
9 p.m.
Government House
Nassau, Bahamas

Jonathan Hanson rang the doorbell to the front door of Government House.

"9:00pm right on time," Oliver Blackwood said, snapping shut his gold pocket watch.

No one answered, and as Hanson reached to ring the bell again, the door swung open. An obviously flustered maid spurted out, "everybody is on the East Terrace watching the fire on Hog Island."

Spinning on her heals she headed into the house. Blackwood and Hanson looked at each other realizing that things were now well under way.

"Follow me," Hanson said, as he started into the foyer of the house, "I have been here twice before; I think I can find the East Patio."

Oliver Blackwood fell in behind his step and together the two men made their way to the east side of the mansion. As they emerged through one of the open louvered doors onto the patio, they were greeted by the backsides of the Duke and Duchess of Windsor, Rolf Wiegard and Nancy and David Atkinson – an image that would stay in Oliver Blackwood's mind forever.

They faced Hog Island, and in the distance one could see a huge fire had lit up the night sky and reflected off of the water to create a picture of a huge ball of flame glowing on the horizon.

Blackwood thought it surreal, it was deadly quiet, not a sound in the air, the fire was too far away to be heard, and those present were stunned into silence.

Jonathan Hanson broke the peace clearing his throat twice; the only one to hear it was his daughter Nancy.

"Oh Daddy, you've arrived," Nancy said as she turned away from the fire toward her father and Oliver Blackwood. This caused the rest of the party, except for Rolf Wiegard, to look away from the fire.

Edward locked eyes with Oliver Blackwood.

They held their gaze until the Governor General looked away, casting a glance in the direction of Rolf Wiegard. Wiegard had was entranced by the fire and had yet to turn and acknowledge the new arrivals.

Edward stiffened and the years of training kicked in. He turned and started forward and with a huge smile on his face as he greeted Hanson and Blackwood.

"Our dear friend Jonathan! How good it is to see you and Sir Oliver Blackwood as well, or has our brother not knighted you yet?"

Blackwood did not respond and Edward did not wait for one.

"Look my dear, our guests have arrived," Edward said, turning toward Wallis.

"Welcome, Jonathan. So good to have you in our home again," Wallis said, offering her hand to Hanson. "Please someone kindly introduce me to the lovely gentleman that you have brought with you."

"My apologies, your Grace I did not realize you had not met. This is Oliver Blackwood, an old friend of the family."

Blackwood caught himself smiling. Jonathan Hanson had referred to Wallis as Your Grace, a title that he reserved for anyone of any official bearing whatsoever. A royal, a clergy member, a judge, a politician, anyone of any official status, was your grace to Jonathan Hanson.

"Welcome to Government House, Mr. Blackwood. Have you ever been here before?" Wallis asked, offering her hand to Blackwood.

"I have been in the Bahamas before but never as a guest at Government House. It is my humble honor to be here," Oliver Blackwood replied, bending his head and kissing Wallis's hand.

"Oh Oliver has been around a long time my dear," Edward said. "Do not fall for his humble routine. We assure you there is very little humbling about Oliver Blackwood."

"Rolf," Edward said, turning to Wiegard. "We have guests. Turn around, man."

With those words Wiegard spun and cried at those assembled.

"Guests! Guests! To hell with your guests, can you not see? Are you that damn dense! Hog Island is on fire and that means you and I are on fire! Do you not see that, you imbecile?"

Wiegard's outburst split the night into a stony silence.

Saturday, November 8th, 1941
9:15 p.m.
Nassau Harbour

Krueger guided the motor launch into Nassau Harbour. He had given the scientists and the guards the larger of Wiegard's two motor launches and he, Nash and Franklyn as well as the two German missiles, made the trip from Hog Island in the smaller of the two crafts.

Krueger and Franklyn worked in unison to dock the launch and Franklyn quickly scrambled ashore and secured all of the mooring lines. They docked the motor launch next to Jonathan Hanson's yacht.

Krueger and Nash faced each other in the center of the launch. The two German missiles lay at their feet under the cover of an old weather beaten blue tarp.

"Well, Mr. Nash. I believe this is where we part. I wish you hadn't killed my radio as you have now created an additional obstacle for me but nevertheless, I appreciate you being on the right side."

"How do you intend to deal with these missiles?" Thomas asked, pointing toward the tarp at their feet.

"I intend to get them into my Navy's hands as soon as possible. What about you, Mr. Nash? Is your mission complete, or am I now going to have to fight you again?"

Thomas smiled.

"No more fighting," he said, extending his hand to the young American. "My mission is not complete – but it has nothing to do with your missiles."

Releasing Krueger's hand, Thomas climbed ashore calling out to the two men.

"Best of luck to ya lads. I'm late for cocktails at Government House."

⚔ ⚔

The tunnel vision began to set in as soon as Thomas left Krueger and Franklyn and began the climb up the hill to Government House. Those treacherous traitorous words that dripped from Edward's mouth much like the bile that was now building in Thomas's throat had doomed His Royal disgraced Highness.

Ascending the hill toward Government House, Thomas knew that Edward's darkest hour was at hand and he wanted to embrace the moment. A church bell struck marking the bottom of the hour and Shakespeare's lines from Macbeth echoed in Thomas's head.

"The bell invites me. Hear it not Duncan, for it is a knell that summons thee to heaven or to hell."

⊷⊱⊰⊶

Saturday, November 8th, 9:30 p.m.
Government House
Nassau, Bahamas

Oliver Blackwood hadn't met Rolf Wiegard in person and at this moment he was witnessing the Swiss industrialist in a complete meltdown.

Edward had met Wiegard's outburst with the stiffness that came from royalty but the rest of the guests were still stunned by Wiegard's ranting and name-calling.

Even Wiegard caught himself, but not before Commissioner Atkinson spoke up.

"Enough! I will not tolerate your disrespect. Control yourself man, show some decorum."

Wiegard's face was the picture of rage and in the center of his forehead a large vein had popped out.

"Rolf, you must relax or you will cause yourself some damage," Wallis said.

Edward, for his part, had not uttered a response.

"Fools! All of you; fools!" Wiegard spit the words out. "I have spent a fortune in time and money for the great cause of returning you to power and for the greatest cause of our lifetime, and you sit here while it all goes up in smoke and tell me to relax."

"I may be able to shed some light on the situation." Blackwood said, as everyone turned to face him.

"The British Government is very aware of what you have been doing on Hog Island and I would venture to say that the fire we see in the distance is justice being served."

"Justice. What the hell do you mean by justice and who the hell are you?" Wiegard said, snarling as he stepped toward Blackwood.

The Commissioner quickly placed himself in Wiegard's path and with a fierceness never displayed before to those gathered, grabbed the irate Wiegard by the front of his jacket, tightened his grip and snarled directly into his face.

"Mr. Blackwood is the Prime Minister's personal friend and your game is over."

Blackwood heard the cocking of a pistol.

⊷+⊶

"The game is over for all of you." His voice was calm and steady as Thomas emerged from the shadows off the east side of the patio. "Your perverted little science experiment is over."

His weapon, drawn and cocked was pointed directly at Wiegard, whom the Commissioner had released and shoved to the side. Wallis gasped as soon as she saw the gun, but Edward remained motionless and silent.

"I am the one who blew up your little laboratory and I am the one who has ruined your plans and now I intend to finish the job I came here to do."

Thomas was aware of Oliver Blackwood's presence but neither man acknowledged the other. It didn't surprise him that Blackwood was present on the island; he knew better than to be caught off guard by the old man.

Edward turned and came face-to-face with Thomas.

"Who in damnation are you?

"I am your justice, your Royal Highness. I am someone who knows the truth and knows what a wretched, treacherous little man you are, a traitor to your country and your King a Nazi stooge, and worst of all a pathetic excuse for an Englishman."

"And you are here to right all of these, eh, perceived evils, as you say?" Edward replied, shifting slightly. "What are you going to do, shoot me in front of all of these witnesses? Do you think a commoner like you can kill a King, let alone survive something like that?

"I would not be killing a King now, would I?" Thomas said, turning the gun on Edward. "You squandered your birthright because of a woman. A woman!

You relinquished your power and then regretted it and your sense of self and importance propelled you to plan to kill thousands upon thousands of innocent people, your people, in an attempt to return you to the throne. And as Hitler's lap dog, no less. No. Killing you would be a great honor and a justice served on the side of humanity."

Thomas's words seemed to have sucked all of the oxygen out of the air and then Rolf Wiegard lunged toward him.

Blackwood, having anticipated Wiegard's temperament, quickly put his leg out, tripping the enraged man who tumbled to the ground.

Thomas released the safety on his weapon and raised the gun so it pointed directly at the center of Edward's head.

The shot rang out, the moment shattered. Wallis and Nancy screamed.

The volley, smoke and smell of gun discharge shocked everyone; Nancy Atkinson was the first to see the blood seeping out of Thomas's chest. With a gasp, the gun fell from his hand and he collapsed vertically to the ground.

From the bushes on the other side of the patio, Krueger emerged with his weapon drawn, still hot from the shot fired.

Commissioner Atkinson was the first to spring into action and he immediately knelt down to check on Thomas, He looked up at the others after searching for a pulse and nodded no, Thomas Nash was dead.

Wiegard picked himself up off of the floor where Oliver Blackwood had tripped him and screamed at Krueger.

"Kill the old man," he said, pointing at Blackwood. "Kill him now!"

In one fell swoop, Commissioner Atkinson's meaty fist slammed Wiegard in the face, knocking him back down on the ground and breaking his nose. Before he could let out the first scream from the pain, the Commissioner kicked him rapidly three times in the chest, breaking his ribs and starving him of enough oxygen to be able to mount a cry.

Krueger had not moved, but he had lowered the gun. He had no intent of shooting anyone else this evening. He spoke directly to Edward.

"My true purpose here was always to protect you. You have President Roosevelt to thank for that, and for the fact that you are still breathing." Then turning to Oliver Blackwood he said, "I know who you are, sir, and I have the missiles that these bastards were building. I need to get them off this island as soon as possible. Can you help me?"

⊨+ +⊨

Oliver Blackwood was as shocked as everyone at Krueger's actions but he quickly concluded that Roosevelt was one step ahead of him. There would be no killing of Edward tonight.

He turned to Commissioner Atkinson.

"I am going to leave you this mess to clean up, secure the Governor General and Mrs. Windsor. I am sure you can handle the staff and the locals."

Then, turning to Krueger and pointing to Wiegard, he said, "Grab this wretched excuse of human waste and bring him down to the harbour. We have a boat there and we will take you, him and the missiles with us. Now, let's get moving."

Krueger, who had put his weapon away, reached down and picked up Wiegard's half-conscious body.

As Jonathan Hanson led the way out of Government House and down towards his yacht, it occurred to Blackwood that his old friend had not spoken during the entire scene.

Blackwood had a feeling that Hanson's real intent was about to be revealed.

CHAPTER THIRTY-THREE

Saturday, November 7th, 1941
10:30 p.m.
Nassau Harbour

Krueger spotted Franklyn sitting between the Launch and Hanson's yacht dangling his feet over the side of the dock. As the group approached the boat, Franklyn sprang to his feet his face frozen in astonishment as Krueger tossed the half-conscious Rolf Wiegard on to the dock.

"You can transfer the missiles to this boat over here," Blackwood said, indicating the yacht docked just two slips away.

"I'm going to get Wiegard aboard and secure first and then I will load the weapons," replied Krueger as he bent down to pick up a still-moaning Wiegard up off the dock.

Franklyn assisted Krueger in hoisting Wiegard aboard the yacht and taking him down below. Krueger could see that Franklyn was fixated on Wiegard's blood-stained face and swollen nose. The man seemed to be struggling to breathe and he made a whistling noise every time he exhaled.

After they had secured their prisoner, Franklyn said. "Where Mr. Nash at?"

"I don't know," Krueger snapped. "And right now I don't have time to worry about it. We need to get those two missiles on board the launch moved over here and we need to do it now. So let's get a move on."

For the moment, the explanation was good enough for Franklyn, but as the boy started up the ladder to the deck, Wiegard coughed and called out.

"Don't trust him, boy. He knows exactly where your friend Nash is. Go ahead and tell him," Wiegard said, nodding toward Krueger. "Tell him you killed his friend and that his body is lying on the verandah of Government House." The words ended in Wiegard gasping for air and coughing up more blood as he tried to add something else, but Krueger was out of patience.

"Move, boy. This son of a bitch doesn't know what he is saying and he is desperate to escape from here. We need to get those damn weapons moved over here and I'm sure Nash will show up."

Franklyn scurried up the ladder followed by Krueger and they quickly made their way over to the launch.

⟞⟞ ⟝⟝

Krueger hated lying to the boy but he knew it was the only thing he could do at the moment. They had quickly transferred the missiles to Hanson's yacht and while Franklyn was down below rearranging some things to secure the missiles in place, he went above deck and found Oliver Blackwood smoking a cigarette and staring back up toward Government House.

"The missiles are on board and secure. We need to leave now. I'm pretty sure there are two German submarines on their way here to pick them up and I don't want to wait around for that."

"What makes you so sure that they are on their way at this precise time?"

"Because of this," Krueger replied, pulling the Wiegard's leather journal out of the back of his pants. "If you read this, you will get the whole picture and I have got to tell you, it's a damn scary picture."

He handed the journal to Blackwood who examined the outside of the book carefully before opening it.

"These two missiles we have on board were intended for Washington and New York. Based on the attack date, I'm pretty sure the U-boats are due here any moment to pick up their cargo and complete their mission."

"When did you say the attack date was?" said Blackwood opening the journal.

"I didn't say. But it's December 7th, the same day the Japanese are going to attack Pearl Harbor."

If those had any effect on Oliver Blackwood, he never showed it. Instead he calmly looked at Krueger. "Well then, we best be under way."

Krueger turned to walk away, satisfied that his sense of urgency had been established when Oliver Blackwood said, "About the boy?"

Krueger stopped and turned to face the old man.

"What about him?"

"How much does he know?" Blackwood had closed the journal now and was staring intently at Krueger.

"He doesn't know anything."

"He knows about the missiles, Hog Island. I venture to say he knows more than he should."

Krueger did not like the direction the conversation was headed in.

"I am not going to allow you to harm that boy. He is innocent and there has already been too much killing tonight."

"What do you suggest we do with him, then?"

"Take him with us, I don't know … but I will not allow you to harm him."

The two men stared at each other for what seemed like the longest time until Oliver Blackwood broke the trance.

"Very well. We will take him with us. Baton down, I will tell Jonathan that it is time to push off."

CHAPTER THIRTY-FOUR

Sunday, November 9th
1 a.m.
Jonathan Hanson's yacht
20 miles northwest of Nassau

Oliver Blackwood sat quietly reading, as Jonathan Hanson entered the salon, he closed the book and stood up.

"That boy Franklyn is a pretty good mate," Hanson said. "He's got the helm right now, so let's get down to business."

"And Krueger," Blackwood asked.

"I've got him on lookout since we're running at night. They're good boys, don't worry, we're in good hands.

" Very well then, let's begin, wake him up," Blackwood said.

"With pleasure," Hanson replied, slapping the unconscious Wiegard hard across the face.

Wiegard came to with a jolt and immediately chocked on the dryness of his blood-crusted mouth.

Blackwood waited until he was alert before beginning.

"Do you know where we are, Mr. Wiegard?"

"Aboard a boat, obviously," Wiegard replied, his voice barely audible.

"You are correct. Except this boat happens to be dead center in the middle of the Tongue of the Ocean, 20,0000 fathoms deep or something like that, and that is where we are going to deposit your soul."

Wiegard smiled and attempted to shift in his chair, straining against the ropes that bound him.

"May I have a glass of water?"

"No, you may not."

"Really, Mr. Blackwood? Every condemned man gets a last wish and since it seems you have appointed yourself both judge and executioner, I would like a glass of water."

Hanson had taken a chair and positioned it next to Rolf Wiegard. He had turned it around and now sat straddling it like a motorcycle just one foot from Wiegard's face.

Placing another chair directly in front of Wiegard, Blackwood said, "There are no rules here, Mr. Wiegard.

You have no last rights. You squandered all good will and all tenants of human decency when you decided to throw in with a monster and develop a weapon that would kill thousands of innocent people. No, Mr. Wiegard, you do not deserve even a glass of water. What I am contemplating right now is exactly how to render your body to the deep. Do I just throw you overboard, tied up as you are, and watch you drown? Or do I gut you and throw you in alive but bleeding and let the sharks chew you to death. What would you do to a man like you, Mr. Wiegard?"

Rolf Wiegard looked through his one open and bloodshot eye and growled.

"What is it you want, Mr. Blackwood?"

"To see you suffer before you die."

Wiegard smiled.

"Then you have achieved your desire."

"Not quite."

"What more can I give you? Wiegard rasped. "You have me tied up on your boat and are promising to feed me to the sharks. All my plans are destroyed and you have my missiles. This is not enough suffering for you?"

Blackwood allowed a few moments of silence to pass before responding.

"I have thought long and hard about this, Mr. Wiegard, and I have come to a couple of conclusions. First, death is too good and too easy a punishment for you and second, to really hurt you, I will have to take your money."

"You are doing this for some money? I don't understand. You are a man of money, why do you need mine?"

"It's not just your money, Mr. Wiegard; it's everything. We want your company, your patents, your trade secrets, your intellectual property, and your government contracts. In other words, Mr. Wiegard, we want everything your father and you built. And then, after we have all of it, I am going to turn you over to the American Government."

Rolf Wiegard started to laugh, but his physical state caused his laughter to erupt into a coughing spasm. When he finally gained his composure, he addressed both men.

"You gentlemen are truly the real criminals here, not I."

"No," Blackwood said. "We are the winners and you are the loser, Mr. Wiegard."

Wiegard went through another coughing fit.

"What about him?" he nodded in the direction of Jonathan Hanson.

"What about him?" Blackwood replied.

"What does he get out of it? After all it seems you are the mastermind behind destroying Hog Island."

Jonathan Hanson began to answer when Oliver Blackwood interrupted.

"Allow me, Jonathan," Blackwood said. "Mr. Wiegard, I used to be an admirer of your work. I am very aware of the technologies and inventions you have developed and quite frankly, I always thought you a brilliant scientist but I never took you for the fool you have become. You may have a brilliant mind but you are lacking a soul and you deserve to be stripped of everything you have. After all, you are complicit in the planning of mass murder, you have thrown in with the greatest tyrant the world has ever known and you will be punished for such blatant criminal and immoral acts."

"Fool. You think me the fool?" Wiegard coughed again. "Hitler is the greatest man this world has ever produced. I may not survive this little episode but I venture to say neither will you.' Turning toward Blackwood, he continued. "And when the Fuhrer conquers your pathetic tiny little diseased ridden island you will remember me and I will have the last laugh."

Oliver Blackwood smiled.

"I venture to say that for all of your intelligence, you still have not grasped the truth in this situation. Maybe you're not thinking clearly as a result of this evening's activities, but you sir are the one who just won this war for us and defeated that little corporal you so fawn over."

Wiegard looked confused for the first time and opened his mouth to speak, but his throat was too dry and raw and he only produced a guttering sound.

Oliver Blackwood walked over to the bar and poured a glass of water, holding it to Wiegard's lips allowing the man to drink half the glass.

"Thank you," Wiegard muttered after drinking the water and glancing toward Hanson who had moved to the other side of the salon and was standing next to the bar.

Wiegard, refreshed, addressed Blackwood.

"How did I just win this war for your side?"

"Simply put, you have just given the Americans the reason they need to get into this fight. By doing so, you have condemned Hitler and Germany to defeat."

A long moment of silence passed.

"I believe it would be most fitting to release you to the Germans," he continued. "You know how Herr Hitler deals with failure and disappointment. Your fate would be one of pain, destruction and death, but my friend here," pointing toward Jonathan Hanson, "and the American Government have other plans for you, your companies and your money."

Oliver Blackwood returned to his chair and Rolf Wiegard stared straight ahead for a few moments before responding.

"Why say anything? Why tell him?"

"To whom are you referring?" asked Blackwood.

"Roosevelt. Why tell him anything?"

"Your point is?"

"The only people who know what Japan has planned for December 7th are the people aboard this boat. If you do not warn the Americans, the Japanese will attack the naval fleet in Hawaii and Roosevelt will then have all of the ammunition he needs to throw America into this conflict. This is, after all, what your goal is: to get America into this war to save your pathetic little empire, which incidentally, will be destroyed one way or the other. Regardless of the outcome of this conflict."

Blackwood tilted his head toward Hanson, who had moved from the bar to stand directly in front of Wiegard. Blackwood was not going to answer that question, but it had actually occurred to him.

Andrew Hanson cast a quick glance at Oliver Blackwood and then with his right fist smashed Rolf Wiegard directly between the eyes, knocking him unconscious.

Turning to face his old friend, Hanson said, "You probably know this already Oliver, but I'm Jewish by birth. Hanson is the name my father chose to protect us from discrimination. That is the reason I came on this trip – so I could hurt one of these Aryan bastards.

Oliver Blackwood smiled to himself. Hanson was probably the only man in the world who could get away with keeping a secret from him.

CHAPTER THIRTY-SIX

June 6th, 2013

Katherine Blackwood's garage

Katherine stood opposite Nicholas. "You look a bit muddled?"

"I'm just sorting it all out," Nicholas replied. "I mean was Krueger working for Wiegard or Roosevelt?"

"Krueger was Roosevelt's man. Remember, the King had asked the President to keep an eye on his brother and Roosevelt was able to place Krueger into the situation.

"So Krueger was really working for the Americans?"

"He was an American."

"And what happened to him?"

"You're beating around the bush and not asking the question you want to ask."

Nicholas smiled before answering, as he felt a little of the schoolteacher in her reappear. She was right, so he decided to get right down to it.

"Your grandfather, Jonathan Hanson, Wiegard and Krueger, along with Franklyn, who may or may not have known, were the only people who had the knowledge that Japan was planning to bomb Pearl Harbor on December 7th."

"Go on," said Katherine.

"Japan bombed Pearl Harbor which means the men on that yacht didn't do anything to stop it. My question is, did they allow this to happen or did they present the President with the evidence and did he allow it to happen? And if that is the case, how did these men keep such a secret for such a long time?"

Katherine did not answer for a few minutes. The time allowed the gravity of Nicholas's question to settle in; he had, after all, come to the crux of the matter.

"Before I give you a direct answer to that question," she began. "I will tell you the fate of all of those aboard the yacht that evening."

Nicholas shifted his stance in anticipation that all of the great secrets that Katherine had so dearly guarded all of these years were about to come out.

"As for my Grandfather and Franklyn, you know most of the story. Were Franklyn not such an innocent boy of sixteen I am quite certain that my Grandfather would have killed him and dumped his body overboard. That might sound shocking, but my Grandfather was ruthless. He chose however to save Franklyn's life but he knew that Franklyn could never return to The Bahamas. So he brought him here to England and he has been here ever since."

Katherine paused and took a sip of tea before continuing.

"And then there was the esteemed Mr. Rolf Wiegard. The Americans wanted him alive, so he survived. Jonathan Hanson took ninety percent of Wiegard's holdings leaving him a mere ten percent of his own company but it was more than enough to live out a nice quiet life in Virginia."

"You mean that he didn't even go to jail or anything?" asked Nicholas. "That is unbelievable that the Americans would let him survive knowing what he was up to ... I don't understand."

"The Americans are a strange lot, I must admit," Katherine said. "You see, they felt that Wiegard could be of use he was after all a brilliant engineer and designer and so they allowed him to live peacefully under an assumed name in the Virginia countryside. He was even able to bring his family over and he became a consultant and through the company now controlled by Hanson, worked on most of America's secret military applications almost up to the day he died."

"So Hanson doubles his fortune, takes Wiegard's company from him, turns around and employs him as a consultant to make him even more money, specifically off of the American armed services ... Wow."

"That young man is the American capitalist system in a nutshell. Where there is money to be made, it will be made. I cannot say I always agree with it but I must admit I do admire that uniquely American attitude of free enterprise."

"And Krueger?"

"I told you my Grandfather could be ruthless, well after the little conversation with Wiegard below deck, Hanson and My Grandfather went above deck and sent Franklyn below to keep an eye on the still tied up and unconscious Wiegard. While Jonathan Hanson took the wheel, My Grandfather walked up to Krueger who was staring out to sea and shot him in the back of the head causing his body to fall overboard."

Katherine paused for a moment and then continued. "My Grandfather told me that Krueger understood his fate because he didn't even turn around as he came up behind him and shot him dead."

Neither Katherine nor Nicholas spoke. Each was engrossed in their own thoughts until Nicholas finally broke the silence.

"Krueger was expendable?" Nicholas said.

"Something like that," Katherine replied.

"And then there were two."

"Yes. My Grandfather and Jonathan Hanson."

"The spy master and the profiteer. Did they tell Roosevelt or did these two ruthless men, as you say, let Pearl Harbor happen?"

Walking over to Andrew Stone's desk Katherine retrieved a piece of paper that she handed to Nicholas. It was a hand-written note on very fine stationary and embossed with the words "The White House."

He looked over at Katherine who had retaken her seat and then began to read the short note.

November 17th, 1941

My dearest friend Winston,

The destiny of the American and British people has been and will forever be intertwined. Those of us who carry the torch of freedom and the love of God are destined to preserve that freedom and see that his will be done on earth.

The agonizing dilemma and the terrible truth that we face today compel us to rely on providence and seek his guidance in what we do. I pray for the souls of the innocent that we are about to condemn and I take these deaths into my heart and doom my humanity as homage to theirs.

We will stand with you against tyranny and oppression. Freedom must survive for the grace of God, the love of mankind and the future of the world.

God bless and keep you.

Franklin Delano Roosevelt.

Nicholas allowed his finger to trace over the name Franklin that was signed in blue ink having no doubt as to the author's authenticity.

"I assure you the signature belongs to Roosevelt," Katherine said. "The President wrote that note out in front of my Grandfather and gave it to him to personally deliver to Churchill. He decided to let the attack on Hawaii happen."

Nicholas thought for a few moments before responding. "So your grandfather revealed everything to the President. I am little surprised by that, to tell you the truth. He didn't need to say anything he could have just let Pearl Harbor happen. It would have gotten America into the war; he would have protected Roosevelt and accomplished what Britain needed, America fighting in the war. It seems to me that would be more in fitting with the type of man your Grandfather was."

"I can see where you would think that, but understand my Grandfather knew that Roosevelt was looking for a way to get into the war and would need something as horrible as Pearl Harbor to bring his fellow countrymen around to the idea. He also knew that the President was made of the right stuff and had the strength to make the right decision. I spoke to him at length about his decision to tell Roosevelt and my Grandfather told me that he personally could not bear to have had those innocent deaths at Pearl Harbor on his hands alone. As he put it, the burden was too great for one man to bear so he, Churchill and ultimately, Roosevelt all took this great sin to their graves.

"It was a sin, wasn't it?" Nicholas began, "I mean… it was mass murder. Three thousand some American sailors died at Pearl Harbor that day."

"The few were sacrificed to save the many," she replied. "It was a horrid situation to be in, but as I have told you, these men had the strength to do what needed to be done to save the world."

"It's ironic, don't you think?" Nicholas asked.

"What do you mean?"

"What I mean is, Churchill condemned Edward yet Roosevelt saved him."

Katherine smiled, her reluctance evident. "The ultimate case of the new world saving the old world and, Roosevelt was royalty."

Nicholas sat in silence for a long time running everything over and over again in his mind. He still had questions, but he understood the story and how everything had happened. Churchill had ordered the murder of a King, Roosevelt had known about the Japanese intent to bomb Pearl Harbor and thus sacrificed thousands of American sailors and this woman sitting in front of him had spent her life keeping these secrets hidden.

The longer he thought about it the more he realized that Katherine was correct. These men were great men because as horrifying as their actions were, the result was; Britain and the world survived the tyranny of the

Nazi state. He felt his perception of the war, and of those who led the great fight against tyranny, changed forever.

However, he still was not sure what his role on all of this was.

Nicholas realized there were still a few loose ends.

"Tell me, what happened with the Commissioner and Nancy Atkinson?"

"Well as you know, the Commissioner and my Grandfather had a history together, and Churchill knew Atkinson as well. The Commissioner cleaned up the mess that was left in Nassau. He secured Edward and Wallis, disposed of Nash's remains and basically silenced the staff at Government House, along with any other rumors or loose talk. The Atkinsons stayed in the Bahamas until the end of the war and then moved to Boston where they lived out their lives.

The Commissioner died in 1951 at the young age of seventy-four and Nancy lived right up until 1981. She died one of the wealthiest women in the world, thanks to her father and to Rolf Wiegard, whose fortune she also controlled. They never had any children and all of the money was left to charity upon her death.

"So Nash was disposed of, like Krueger. Churchill had been right; he was expendable." Nicholas said to himself.

"Yes," Katherine answered in a low voice. "He was expendable."

And, after a long pause, she whispered, "Just like your father was."

His father had not come up in a while but he knew he was at the center of this story.

He had been so engrossed in the tale about Hog Island that he had not thought about him in the last few hours or his connection to all of this. He looked Katherine directly in the eyes and spoke.

"I imagine that the time has now come for you to tell me the truth about my father and the truth about his death?"

"Yes," she replied, meeting his gaze. "It seems we have reached that point."

Katherine hesitated for a few moments. She rose from her seat and moved again to Andrew Stone's desk on the other side of the garage, retrieving a dark red dossier she turned to Nicholas.

"This file contains the story of your father's life and death. It holds the last of the sins that I have spent a lifetime guarding. Through the years, I have taken comfort in my solitude but Time has escaped me." A reluctant smile crossed her lips. "I brought you here this night to tell you this story to impress upon you the greatness of these poor wretched souls who had the fortitude to do the unthinkable."

Katherine paused and took a long look around the garage.

"Your father was the love of my life and a great man in the same sense as Churchill and Roosevelt and, yes, even my Grandfather. He was patriotic and loyal and possessed the same qualities of honor and fate that they possessed. It is my hope that by making this so personal for you, you will treat these men, your father included, with dignity and respect and that the love of a son for a father will guide your decisions."

Katherine paused and turned the file around and handed it to Nicholas. She looked out of the window, at the back of the garage. Nicholas noticed that dawn had broken and the sun was rising.

"Morning has broken," She began, "and I am going to bed. Franklyn will be in shortly and he will make a fresh pot of tea and some breakfast. I imagine you will be here when I awake and I look forward to speaking with you then."

With those words, Katherine leaned over, kissed Nicholas on the forehead and left the garage.

Nicholas slowly approached his father's desk. Placing the file on top, he took a seat in his father's chair and looked around the garage. Leaning back, he allowed himself to imagine his father's world and all of the things that drove him.

Katherine had given him a glimpse into his father's life and what was in the folder would tell him even more, and for that he was grateful. She was giving him back his father.

He closed his eyes in anticipation of what he was about to read.

After a few moments, he opened them and looked at the out side of the file. It was blank.

His fingers hesitated as he opened the folder.

The words, centered in the middle of the page, jumped out at him.

August 31st, 1997
The Assassination of Diana, Princess of Wales.

ABOUT THE AUTHOR

John Kallergis was born in Canton, Ohio and raised in the Bahamas. He lives and teaches In Miami Florida. He is a graduate of the University of Miami and is a passionate storyteller. He has a fascination for World War II history and an overactive imagination.